CONTENTS

from *Sonnets from the Portuguese*

XLIII

How do I love thee? Let me count the ways.
I love thee to the depth and breadth and height
My soul can reach, when feeling out of sight
For the ends of Being and Ideal Grace.
I love thee to the level of every day's
Most quiet need, by sun and candlelight.
I love thee freely, as men strive for Right;
I love thee purely, as they turn from Praise;
I love thee with the passion put to use
In my old griefs, and with my childhood's faith;
I love thee with a love I seemed to lose
With my lost saints, – I love thee with the breath,
Smiles, tears, of all my life! – and, if God choose,
I shall but love thee better after death.

ELIZABETH BARRETT BROWNING

from *Sonnets from the Portuguese*

XIV

If thou must love me, let it be for nought
Except for love's sake only. Do not say
'I love her for her smile . . . her look . . . her way
Of speaking gently, . . . for a trick of thought
That falls in well with mine, and certes brought
A sense of pleasant ease on such a day' –
For these things in themselves, Beloved, may
Be changed, or change for thee,
                                        –and love so wrought,
May be unwrought so. Neither love me for
Thine own dear pity's wiping my cheeks dry,
A creature might forget to weep, who bore
Thy comfort long, and lose thy love thereby.

But love me for love's sake, that evermore
Thou may'st love on through love's eternity.

ELIZABETH BARRETT BROWNING

Meeting at Night

The grey sea and the long black land;
And the yellow half-moon large and low;
And the startled little waves that leap
In fiery ringlets from their sleep,
As I gain the cove with pushing prow,
And quench its speed i' the slushy sand.

Then a mile of warm sea-scented beach;
Three fields to cross till a farm appears;
A tap at the pane, the quick sharp scratch
And blue spurt of a lighted match,
And a voice less loud, thro' its joys and fears,
Than the two hearts beating each to each!

ROBERT BROWNING

'How still, how happy!'

How still, how happy! Those are words
That once would scarce agree together;
I loved the plashing of the surge,
The changing heaven, the breezy weather,

More than smooth seas and cloudless skies
And solemn, soothing, softened airs
That in the forest woke no sighs
And from the green spray shook no tears.

How still, how happy! Now I feel
Where silence dwells is sweeter far
Than laughing mirth's most joyous swell
However pure its raptures are.

Come, sit down on this sunny stone:
'Tis wintry light o'er flowerless moors –
But sit – for we are all alone
And clear expand heaven's breathless shores.

I could think in the withered grass
Spring's budding wreaths we might discern;
The violet's eye might shyly flash
And young leaves shoot among the fern.

It is but thought – full many a night
The snow shall clothe those hills afar
And storms shall add a drearier blight
And winds shall wage a wilder war,

Before the lark may herald in
Fresh foliage twined with blossoms fair
And summer days again begin
Their glory-haloed crown to wear.

Yet my heart loves December's smile
As much as July's golden beam;
Then let us sit and watch the while
The blue ice curdling on the stream.

EMILY JANE BRONTË

Two in the Campagna

I wonder do you feel to-day
   As I have felt since, hand in hand,
We sat down on the grass, to stray
   In spirit better through the land,
This morn of Rome and May?

For me, I touched a thought, I know,
   Has tantalized me many times,
(Like turns of thread the spiders throw
   Mocking across our path) for rhymes
To catch at and let go.

Help me to hold it! First it left
    The yellowing fennel, run to seed
There, branching from the brickwork's cleft,
    Some old tomb's ruin: yonder weed
Took up the floating weft,

Where one small orange cup amassed
    Five beetles, – blind and green they grope
Among the honey-meal: and last,
    Everywhere on the grassy slope
I traced it. Hold it fast!

The champaign with its endless fleece
    Of feathery grasses everywhere!
Silence and passion, joy and peace,
    An everlasting wash of air –
Rome's ghost since her decease.

Such life here, through such lengths of hours,
    Such miracles performed in play,
Such primal naked forms of flowers,
    Such letting nature have her way
While heaven looks from its towers!

How say you? Let us, O my dove,
    Let us be unashamed of soul,
As earth lies bare to heaven above!
    How is it under our control!
To love or not to love?

I would that you were all to me,
    You that are just so much, no more.
Nor yours nor mine, nor slave nor free!
    Where does the fault lie? What the core
O' the wound, since wound must be?

I would I could adopt your will,
    See with your eyes, and set my heart
Beating by yours, and drink my fill
    At your soul's springs, – your part my part
In life, for good and ill.

No. I yearn upward, touch you close,
  Then stand away. I kiss your cheek,
Catch your soul's warmth, – I pluck the rose
  And love it more than tongue can speak –
Then the good minute goes.

Already how am I so far
  Out of that minute? Must I go
Still like the thistle-ball, no bar,
  Onward, whenever light winds blow
Fixed by no friendly star?

Just when I seemed about to learn!
  Where is the thread now? Off again!
The old trick! Only I discern –
  Infinite passion, and the pain
Of finite hearts that yearn.

ROBERT BROWNING

The Bluebell

The Bluebell is the sweetest flower
  That waves in summer air:
Its blossoms have the mightiest power
  To soothe my spirit's care.

There is a spell in purple heath
  Too wildly, sadly dear;
The violet has a fragrant breath,
  But fragrance will not cheer.

The trees are bare, the sun is cold,
  And seldom, seldom seen;
The heavens have lost their zone of gold,
  And earth her robe of green.

And ice upon the glancing stream
  Has cast its sombre shade;
And distant hills and valleys seem
  In frozen mist arrayed.

The Bluebell cannot charm me now,
    The heath has lost its bloom;
The violets in the glen below,
    They yield no sweet perfume.

But, though I mourn the sweet Bluebell,
    'Tis better far away;
I know how fast my tears would swell
    To see it smile to-day.

For, oh! when chill the sunbeams fall
    Adown that dreary sky,
And gild yon dank and darkened wall
    With transient brilliancy;

How do I weep, how do I pine
    For the time of flowers to come,
And turn me from that fading shine,
    To mourn the fields of home!

EMILY JANE BRONTË

'Mild the mist upon the hill'

Mild the mist upon the hill
Telling not of storms to-morrow;
No; the day has wept its fill,
Spent its store of silent sorrow.

Oh, I'm gone back to the days of youth,
I am a child once more;
And 'neath my father's sheltering roof,
And near the old hall door,

I watch this cloudy evening fall,
After a day of rain:
Blue mists, sweet mists of summer pall
The horizon's mountain-chain.

The damp stands in the long, green grass
As thick as morning's tears;
And dreamy scents of fragrance pass
That breathe of other years.

EMILY JANE BRONTË

Grief

I tell you, hopeless grief is passionless;
That only men incredulous of despair,
Half-taught in anguish, through the midnight air
Beat upward to God's throne in loud access
Of shrieking and reproach. Full desertness,
In souls as countries, lieth silent-bare
Under the blanching, vertical eye-glare
Of the absolute Heavens. Deep-hearted man, express
Grief for thy Dead in silence like to death –
Most like a monumental statue set
In everlasting watch and moveless woe
Till itself crumble to the dust beneath.
Touch it; the marble eyelids are not wet:
If it could weep, it could arise and go.

ELIZABETH BARRETT BROWNING

'No coward soul is mine'

No coward soul is mine
No trembler in the world's storm-troubled sphere
I see Heaven's glories shine
And Faith shines equal arming me from Fear

O God within my breast
Almighty ever-present Deity
Life, that in me hast rest
As I Undying Life, have power in thee

Vain are the thousand creeds
That move men's hearts, unutterably vain,
Worthless as withered weeds
Or idlest froth amid the boundless main

To waken doubt in one
Holding so fast by thy infinity
So surely anchored on
The steadfast rock of Immortality

With wide-embracing love
Thy spirit animates eternal years
Pervades and broods above,
Changes, sustains, dissolves, creates and rears

Though Earth and moon were gone
And suns and universes ceased to be
And thou wert left alone
Every Existence would exist in thee

There is not room for Death
Nor atom that his might could render void
Since thou art Being and Breath
And what thou art may never be destroyed.

EMILY JANE BRONTË

Death Sweet

Is it not sweet to die? for, what is death,
But sighing that we ne'er may sigh again,
Getting a length beyond our tedious selves;
But trampling the last tear from poisonous sorrow,
Spilling our woes, crushing our frozen hopes,
And passing like an incense out of man?
Then, if the body felt, what were its sense,
Turning to daisies gently in the grave,
If not the soul's most delicate delight

8

When it does filtrate, through the pores of thought,
In love and the enamelled flowers of song?

THOMAS LOVELL BEDDOES

Memorabilia

Ah, did you once see Shelley plain,
     And did he stop and speak to you
And did you speak to him again?
     How strange it seems and new!

But you were living before that,
     And also you are living after;
And the memory I started at –
     My starting moves your laughter.

I crossed a moor, with a name of its òwn
     And a certain use in the world no doubt,
Yet a hand's-breadth of it shines alone
     'Mid the blank miles round about:

For there I picked up on the heather
     And there I put inside my breast
A moulted feather, an eagle-feather!
     Well, I forget the rest.

ROBERT BROWNING

'I remember, I remember'

I remember, I remember,
The house where I was born,
The little window where the sun
Came peeping in at morn;
He never came a wink too soon,
Nor brought too long a day,
But now, I often wish the night
Had borne my breath away!

I remember, I remember,
The roses, red and white,
The violets, and the lily-cups,
Those flowers made of light!
The lilacs where the robin built,
And where my brother set
The laburnum on his birthday, –
The tree is living yet!

I remember, I remember,
Where I was used to swing,
And thought the air must rush as fresh
To swallows on the wing;
My spirit flew in feathers then,
That is so heavy now,
And summer pools could hardly cool
The fever on my brow!

I remember, I remember,
The fir trees dark and high;
I used to think their slender tops
Were close against the sky:
It was a childish ignorance,
But now 'tis little joy
To know I'm farther off from heaven
Than when I was a boy.

THOMAS HOOD

To Flush, My Dog

Loving friend, the gift of one
Who her own true faith has run
    Through thy lower nature,
Be my benediction said
With my hand upon thy head,
    Gentle fellow-creature!

Like a lady's ringlets brown,
Flow thy silken ears adown
   Either side demurely
Of thy silver-suited breast
Shining out from all the rest
   Of thy body purely.

Darkly brown thy body is,
Till the sunshine striking this
   Alchemize its dulness,
When the sleek curls manifold
Flash all over into gold
   With a burnished fulness.

Underneath my stroking hand,
Startled eyes of hazel bland
   Kindling, growing larger,
Up thou leapest with a spring,
Full of prank and curveting,
   Leaping like a charger.

Leap! thy broad tail waves a light,
Leap! thy slender feet are bright,
   Canopied in fringes;
Leap! those tasselled ears of thine
Flicker strangely, fair and fine
   Down their golden inches.

Yet, my pretty, sportive friend,
Little is't to such an end
   That I praise thy rareness;
Other dogs may be thy peers
Haply in these drooping ears
   And this glossy fairness.

But of *thee* it shall be said,
This dog watched beside a bed
   Day and night unweary,
Watched within a curtained room
Where no sunbeam brake the gloom
   Round the sick and dreary.

Roses, gathered for a vase,
In that chamber died apace,
  Beam and breeze resigning;
This dog only, waited on,
Knowing that when light is gone
  Love remains for shining.

Other dogs in thymy dew
Tracked the hares and followed through
  Sunny moor or meadow;
This dog only, crept and crept
Next a languid cheek that slept,
  Sharing in the shadow.

Other dogs of loyal cheer
Bounded at the whistle clear,
  Up the woodside hieing;
This dog only, watched in reach
Of a faintly uttered speech
  Or a louder sighing.

And if one or two quick tears
Dropped upon his glossy ears
  Or a sigh came double,
Up he sprang in eager haste,
Fawning, fondling, breathing fast,
  In a tender trouble.

And this dog was satisfied
If a pale thin hand would glide
  Down his dewlaps sloping, –
Which he pushed his nose within,
After, – platforming his chin
  On the palm left open.

This dog, if a friendly voice
Call him now to blither choice
  Than such chamber-keeping,
'Come out!' praying from the door, –
Presseth backward as before,
  Up against me leaping.

Therefore to this dog will I,
Tenderly not scornfully,
   Render praise and favour:
With my hand upon his head,
Is my benediction said
   Therefore and for ever.

And because he loves me so,
Better than his kind will do
   Often man or woman,
Give I back more love again
Than dogs often take of men,
   Leaning from my Human.

Blessings on thee, dog of mine,
Pretty collars make thee fine,
   Sugared milk make fat thee!
Pleasures wag on in thy tail,
Hands of gentle motion fail
   Nevermore, to pat thee!

Downy pillow take thy head,
Silken coverlid bestead,
   Sunshine help thy sleeping!
No fly's buzzing wake thee up,
No man break thy purple cup
   Set for drinking deep in.

Whiskered cats arointed flee,
Sturdy stoppers keep from thee
   Cologne distillations;
Nuts lie in thy path for stones,
And thy feast-day macaroons
   Turn to daily rations!

Mock I thee, in wishing weal?
Tears are in my eyes to feel
   Thou art made so straitly,
Blessing needs must straiten too, –
Little canst thou joy or do,
   Thou who lovest *greatly*.

Yet be blessed to the height
Of all good and all delight
    Pervious to thy nature;
Only *loved* beyond that line,
With a love that answers thine,
    Loving fellow-creature!

ELIZABETH BARRETT BROWNING

Love in a Life

Room after room,
I hunt the house through
We inhabit together.
Heart, fear nothing, for, heart, thou shalt find her –
Next time, herself! – not the trouble behind her
Left in the curtain, the couch's perfume!
As she brushed it, the cornice-wreath blossomed anew:
Yon looking-glass gleamed at the wave of her feather.

Yet the day wears,
And door succeeds door;
I try the fresh fortune –
Range the wide house from the wing to the centre.
Still the same chance! she goes out as I enter.
Spend my whole day in the quest, – who cares?
But 't is twilight, you see, – with such suites to explore,
Such closets to search, such alcoves to importune!

ROBERT BROWNING

from *The Princess*

Now sleeps the crimson petal, now the white;
Nor waves the cypress in the palace walk;
Nor winks the gold fin in the porphyry font:
The fire-fly wakens: waken thou with me.

Now droops the milkwhite peacock like a ghost,
And like a ghost she glimmers on to me.

Now lies the Earth all Danaë to the stars,
And all thy heart lies open unto me.

Now slides the silent meteor on, and leaves
A shining furrow, as thy thoughts in me.

Now folds the lily all her sweetness up,
And slips into the bosom of the lake:
So fold thyself, my dearest, thou, and slip
Into my bosom and be lost in me.

ALFRED, LORD TENNYSON

My Last Duchess

FERRARA

That's my last Duchess painted on the wall,
Looking as if she were alive. I call
That piece a wonder, now: Frà Pandolf's hands
Worked busily a day, and there she stands.
Will't please you sit and look at her? I said
'Frà Pandolf' by design, for never read
Strangers like you that pictured countenance,
The depth and passion of its earnest glance,
But to myself they turned (since none puts by
The curtain I have drawn for you, but I)
And seemed as they would ask me, if they durst,
How such a glance came there; so, not the first
Are you to turn and ask thus. Sir, 't was not
Her husband's presence only, called that spot
Of joy into the Duchess' cheek: perhaps
Frà Pandolf chanced to say 'Her mantle laps
'Over my lady's wrist too much,' or 'Paint
'Must never hope to reproduce the faint
'Half-flush that dies along her throat': such stuff
Was courtesy, she thought, and cause enough

For calling up that spot of joy. She had
A heart – how shall I say? – too soon made glad,
Too easily impressed; she liked whate'er
She looked on, and her looks went everywhere
Sir, 'twas all one! My favour at her breast,
The dropping of the daylight in the West,
The bough of cherries some officious fool
Broke in the orchard for her, the white mule
She rode with round the terrace – all and each
Would draw from her alike the approving speech,
Or blush, at least. She thanked men, – good! but thanked
Somehow – I know not how – as if she ranked
My gift of a nine-hundred-years-old name
With anybody's gift. Who'd stoop to blame
This sort of trifling? Even had you skill
In speech – (which I have not) – to make your will
Quite clear to such an one, and say, 'Just this
Or that in you disgusts me; here you miss,
Or there exceed the mark' – and if she let
Herself be lessoned so, nor plainly set
Her wits to yours, forsooth, and made excuse,
– E'en then would be some stooping; and I choose
Never to stoop. Oh sir, she smiled, no doubt,
Whene'er I passed her; but who passed without
Much the same smile? This grew; I gave commands;
Then all smiles stopped together. There she stands
As if alive. Will't please you rise? We'll meet
The company below, then. I repeat,
The Count your master's known munificence
Is ample warrant that no just pretence
Of mine for dowry will be disallowed;
Though his fair daughter's self, as I avowed
At starting, is my object. Nay, we'll go
Together down, sir. Notice Neptune, though,
Taming a sea-horse, thought a rarity,
Which Claus of Innsbruck cast in bronze for me!

ROBERT BROWNING

from *The Prisoner*

A FRAGMENT

He comes with western winds, with evening's wandering airs,
With that clear dusk of heaven that brings the thickest stars.
Winds take a pensive tone, and stars a tender fire,
And visions rise, and change, that kill me with desire.

Desire for nothing known in my maturer years,
When Joy grew mad with awe, at counting future tears.
When, if my spirit's sky was full of flashes warm,
I knew not whence they came, from sun, or thunder storm.

But, first, a hush of peace – a soundless calm descends;
The struggle of distress, and fierce impatience ends.
Mute music soothes my breast, unuttered harmony,
That I could never dream, till Earth was lost to me.

Then dawns the Invisible; the Unseen its truth reveals;
My outward sense is gone my inward essence feels:
Its wings are almost free – its home, its harbour found,
Measuring the gulph, it stoops, and dares the final bound.

Oh, dreadful is the check – intense the agony –
When the ear begins to hear, and the eye begins to see;
When the pulse begins to throb, the brain to think again,
The soul to feel the flesh, and the flesh to feel the chain.

Yet I would lose no sting, would wish no torture less,
The more that anguish racks, the earlier it will bless;
And robed in fires of hell, or bright with heavenly shine,
If it but herald death, the vision is divine!

EMILY JANE BRONTË

from *Idylls of the King: Merlin and Vivien*

In Love, if Love be Love, if Love be ours,
Faith and unfaith can ne'er be equal powers:
Unfaith in aught is want of faith in all.

It is the little rift within the lute,
That by and by will make the music mute,
And ever widening slowly silence all.

The little rift within the lover's lute
Or little pitted speck in garner'd fruit,
That rotting inward slowly moulders all.

It is not worth the keeping: let it go:
But shall it? answer, darling, answer, no.
And trust me not at all or all in all.

ALFRED, LORD TENNYSON

Hope

Hope was but a timid friend;
   She sat without the grated den,
Watching how my fate would tend,
   Even as selfish-hearted men.

She was cruel in her fear;
   Through the bars, one dreary day,
I looked out to see her there,
   And she turned her face away!

Like a false guard, false watch keeping,
   Still in strife, she whispered peace;
She would sing while I was weeping;
   If I listened, she would cease.

False she was, and unrelenting;
   When my last joys strewed the ground,
Even Sorrow saw, repenting,
   Those sad relics scattered round;

Hope, whose whisper would have given
   Balm to all my frenzied pain,
Stretched her wings, and soared to heaven,
   Went, and ne'er returned again!

EMILY JANE BRONTË

The Lost Mistress

All's over, then: does truth sound bitter
    As one at first believes?
Hark, 'tis the sparrows' good-night twitter
    About your cottage eaves!

And the leaf-buds on the vine are woolly,
    I noticed that, today;
One day more bursts them open fully
    —You know the red turns grey.

Tomorrow we meet the same then, dearest?
    May I take your hand in mine?
Mere friends are we, – well, friends the merest
    Keep much that I resign:

For each glance of the eye so bright and black,
    Though I keep with heart's endeavour, –
Your voice, when you wish the snowdrops back,
    Though it stay in my soul for ever! –

Yet I will but say what mere friends say,
    Or only a thought stronger;
I will hold your hand but as long as all may,
    Or so very little longer!

ROBERT BROWNING

Morte d'Arthur

So all day long the noise of battle roll'd
Among the mountains by the winter sea;
Until King Arthur's table, man by man,
Had fall'n in Lyonnesse about their Lord,
King Arthur: then, because his wound was deep,
The bold Sir Bedivere uplifted him,
Sir Bedivere, the last of all his knights,

And bore him to a chapel nigh the field,
A broken chancel with a broken cross,
That stood on a dark strait of barren land.
On one side lay the Ocean, and on one
Lay a great water, and the moon was full.
   Then spake King Arthur to Sir Bedivere:
'The sequel of to-day unsolders all
The goodliest fellowship of famous knights
Whereof this world holds record. Such a sleep
They sleep – the men I loved. I think that we
Shall never more, at any future time,
Delight our souls with talk of knightly deeds,
Walking about the gardens and the halls
Of Camelot, as in the days that were.
I perish by this people which I made, –
Tho' Merlin sware that I should come again
To rule once more – but let what will be, be.
I am so deeply smitten thro' the helm
That without help I cannot last till morn.
Thou therefore take my brand Excalibur,
Which was my pride: for thou rememberest how
In those old days, one summer noon, an arm
Rose up from out the bosom of the lake,
Clothed in white samite, mystic, wonderful,
Holding the sword – and how I row'd across
And took it, and have worn it, like a king:
And, wheresoever I am sung or told
In aftertime, this also shall be known:
But now delay not: take Excalibur,
And fling him far into the middle mere:
Watch what thou seëst, and lightly bring me word.'
   To him replied the bold Sir Bedivere:
'It is not meet, Sir King, to leave thee thus,
Aidless, alone, and smitten thro' the helm.
A little thing may harm a wounded man.
Yet I thy hest will all perform at full,
Watch what I see, and lightly bring thee word.'
   So saying, from the ruin'd shrine he stept

And in the moon athwart the place of tombs,
Where lay the mighty bones of ancient men,
Old knights, and over them the sea-wind sang
Shrill, chill, with flakes of foam. He, stepping down
By zig-zag paths, and juts of pointed rock,
Came on the shining levels of the lake.

There drew he forth the brand Excalibur,
And o'er him, drawing it, the winter moon,
Brightening the skirts of a long cloud, ran forth
And sparkled keen with frost against the hilt:
For all the haft twinkled with diamond sparks,
Myriads of topaz-lights, and jacinth work
Of subtlest jewellery. He gazed so long
That both his eyes were dazzled, as he stood,
This way and that dividing the swift mind,
In act to throw: but at the last it seem'd
Better to leave Excalibur conceal'd
There in the many-knotted waterflags,
That whistled stiff and dry about the marge.
So strode he back slow to the wounded King.

Then spake King Arthur to Sir Bedivere:
'Hast thou perform'd my mission which I gave?
What is it thou hast seen? or what hast heard?'

And answer made the bold Sir Bedivere:
'I heard the ripple washing in the reeds,
And the wild water lapping on the crag.'

To whom replied King Arthur, faint and pale:
'Thou hast betray'd thy nature and thy name,
Not rendering true answer, as beseem'd
Thy fëalty, nor like a noble knight:
For surer sign had follow'd, either hand,
Or voice, or else a motion of the mere.
This is a shameful thing for men to lie.
Yet now, I charge thee, quickly go again
As thou art lief and dear, and do the thing
I bad thee, watch, and lightly bring me word.'

Then went Sir Bedivere the second time
Across the ridge, and paced beside the mere,

Counting the dewy pebbles, fix'd in thought;
But when he saw the wonder of the hilt,
How curiously and strangely chased, he smote
His palms together, and he cried aloud,

'And if indeed I cast the brand away,
Surely a precious thing, one worthy note,
Should thus be lost for ever from the earth,
Which might have pleased the eyes of many men.
What good should follow this, if this were done?
What harm, undone? deep harm to disobey,
Seeing obedience is the bond of rule.
Were it well to obey then, if a king demand
An act unprofitable, against himself?
The King is sick, and knows not what he does.
What record, or what relic of my lord
Should be to aftertime, but empty breath
And rumours of a doubt? but were this kept,
Stored in some treasure-house of mighty kings,
Some one might show it at a joust of arms,
Saying, "King Arthur's sword, Excalibur,
Wrought by the lonely maiden of the Lake,
Nine years she wrought it, sitting in the deeps
Upon the hidden bases of the hills."
So might some old man speak in the aftertime
To all the people, winning reverence.
But how much honour and much fame were lost.'

So spake he, clouded with his own conceit,
And hid Excalibur the second time,
And so strode back slow to the wounded King.

Then spoke King Arthur, breathing heavily:
'What is it thou hast seen? or what hast heard?'

And answer made the bold Sir Bedivere:
'I heard the water lapping on the crag,
And the long ripple washing in the reeds.'

To whom replied King Arthur, much in wrath:
'Ah, miserable and unkind, untrue,
Unknightly, traitor-hearted! Woe is me!
Authority forgets a dying king,

Laid widow'd of the power in his eye
That bow'd the will. I see thee what thou art,
For thou, the latest-left of all my knights,
In whom should meet the offices of all,
Thou wouldst betray me for the precious hilt;
Either from lust of gold, or like a girl
Valuing the giddy pleasure of the eyes.
Yet, for a man may fail in duty twice,
And the third time may prosper, get thee hence:
But, if thou spare to fling Excalibur,
I will arise and slay thee with my hands.'

   Then quickly rose Sir Bedivere, and ran,
And, leaping down the ridges lightly, plunged
Among the bulrush-beds, and clutch'd the sword,
And strongly wheel'd and threw it. The great brand
Made lightnings in the splendour of the moon,
And flashing round and round, and whirl'd in an arch,
Shot like a streamer of the northern morn,
Seen where the moving isles of winter shock
By night, with noises of the northern sea.
So flash'd and fell the brand Excalibur:
But ere he dipt the surface, rose an arm
Clothed in white samite, mystic, wonderful,
And caught him by the hilt, and brandish'd him
Three times, and drew him under in the mere.
And lightly went the other to the King.

   Then spoke King Arthur, drawing thicker breath:
'Now see I by thine eyes that this is done.
Speak out: what is it thou hast heard, or seen?'

   And answer made the bold Sir Bedivere:
'Sir King, I closed mine eyelids, lest the gems
Should blind my purpose, for I never saw,
Nor shall see, here or elsewhere, till I die,
Not tho' I live three lives of mortal men,
So great a miracle as yonder hilt.
Then with both hands I flung him, wheeling him;
But when I look'd again, behold an arm,
Clothed in white samite, mystic, wonderful,

That caught him by the hilt, and brandish'd him
Three times, and drew him under in the mere.'

And answer made King Arthur, breathing hard:
'My end draws nigh: 'tis time that I were gone.
Make broad thy shoulders to receive my weight,
And bear me to the margin; yet I fear
My wound hath taken cold, and I shall die.'

So saying, from the pavement he half rose,
Slowly, with pain, reclining on his arm,
And looking wistfully with wide blue eyes
As in a picture. Him Sir Bedivere
Remorsefully regarded thro' his tears,
And would have spoken, but he found not words,
Then took with care, and kneeling on one knee,
O'er both his shoulders drew the languid hands,
And rising bore him thro' the place of tombs.

But, as he walk'd, King Arthur panted hard,
Like one that feels a nightmare on his bed
When all the house is mute. So sigh'd the King,
Muttering and murmuring at his ear, 'Quick, quick!
I fear it is too late, and I shall die.'
But the other swiftly strode from ridge to ridge,
Clothed with his breath, and looking, as he walk'd,
Larger than human on the frozen hills.
He heard the deep behind him, and a cry
Before. His own thought drove him like a goad.
Dry clash'd his harness in the icy caves
And barren chasms, and all to left and right
The bare black cliff clang'd round him, as he based
His feet on juts of slippery crag that rang
Sharp-smitten with the dint of armed heels –
And on a sudden, lo! the level lake,
And the long glories of the winter moon.

Then saw they how there hove a dusky barge,
Dark as a funeral scarf from stem to stern,
Beneath them; and descending they were ware
That all the decks were dense with stately forms
Black-stoled, black-hooded, like a dream – by these

Three Queens with crowns of gold – and from them rose
A cry that shiver'd to the tingling stars,
And, as it were one voice, an agony
Of lamentation, like a wind, that shrills
All night in a waste land, where no one comes,
Or hath come, since the making of the world.

    Then murmur'd Arthur, 'Place me in the barge,'
And to the barge they came. There those three Queens
Put forth their hands, and took the King, and wept.
But she, that rose the tallest of them all
And fairest, laid his head upon her lap,
And loosed the shatter'd casque, and chafed his hands,
And call'd him by his name, complaining loud,
And dropping bitter tears against his brow
Striped with dark blood: for all his face was white
And colourless, and like the wither'd moon
Smote by the fresh beam of the springing east;
And all his greaves and cuisses dash'd with drops
Of onset; and the light and lustrous curls –
That made his forehead like a rising sun
High from the daïs-throne – were parch'd with dust;
Or, clotted into points and hanging loose,
Mix'd with the knightly growth that fringed his lips.
So like a shatter'd column lay the King;
Not like that Arthur who, with lance in rest,
From spur to plume a star of tournament,
Shot thro' the lists at Camelot, and charged
Before the eyes of ladies and of kings.

    Then loudly cried the bold Sir Bedivere,
'Ah! my Lord Arthur, whither shall I go?
Where shall I hide my forehead and my eyes?
For now I see the true old times are dead,
When every morning brought a noble chance,
And every chance brought out a noble knight.
Such times have been not since the light that led
The holy Elders with the gift of myrrh.
But now the whole ROUND TABLE is dissolved
Which was an image of the mighty world;

And I, the last, go forth companionless,
And the days darken round me, and the years,
Among new men, strange faces, other minds.'

　　And slowly answered Arthur from the barge:
'The old order changeth, yielding place to new,
And God fulfils Himself in many ways,
Lest one good custom should corrupt the world.
Comfort thyself: what comfort is in me?
I have lived my life, and that which I have done
May He within Himself make pure! but thou,
If thou shouldst never see my face again,
Pray for my soul. More things are wrought by prayer
Than this world dreams of. Wherefore, let thy voice
Rise like a fountain for me night and day.
For what are men better than sheep or goats
That nourish a blind life within the brain,
If, knowing God, they lift not hands of prayer
Both for themselves and those who call them friend?
For so the whole round earth is every way
Bound by gold chains about the feet of God.
But now farewell. I am going a long way
With these thou seëst – if indeed I go –
(For all my mind is clouded with a doubt)
To the island-valley of Avilion;
Where falls not hail, or rain, or any snow,
Nor ever wind blows loudly; but it lies
Deep-meadow'd, happy, fair with orchard-lawns
And bowery hollows crown'd with summer sea,
Where I will heal me of my grievous wound.'

　　So said he, and the barge with oar and sail
Moved from the brink, like some full-breasted swan
That, fluting a wild carol ere her death,
Ruffles her pure cold plume, and takes the flood
With swarthy webs. Long stood Sir Bedivere
Look'd one black dot against the verge of dawn,
And on the mere the wailing died away.

ALFRED, LORD TENNYSON

How It Strikes a Contemporary

I only knew one poet in my life:
And this, or something like it, was his way.

   You saw go up and down Valladolid,
A man of mark, to know next time you saw.
His very serviceable suit of black
Was courtly once and conscientious still,
And many might have worn it, though none did:
The cloak, that somewhat shone and showed the threads,
Had purpose, and the ruff, significance.
He walked and tapped the pavement with his cane,
Scenting the world, looking it full in face,
An old dog, bald and blindish, at his heels.
They turned up, now, the alley by the church,
That leads nowhither; now, they breathed themselves
On the main promenade just at the wrong time:
You'd come upon his scrutinizing hat,
Making a peaked shade blacker than itself
Against the single window spared some house
Intact yet with its mouldered Moorish work! –
Or else surprise the ferrel of his stick
Trying the mortar's temper 'tween the chinks
Of some new shop a-building, French and fine.
He stood and watched the cobbler at his trade,
The man who slices lemons into drink,
The coffee-roaster's brazier, and the boys
That volunteer to help him turn its winch.
He glanced o'er books on stalls with half an eye,
And fly-leaf ballads on the vendor's string,
And broad-edge bold-print posters by the wall.
He took such cognizance of men and things,
If any beat a horse, you felt he saw;
If any cursed a woman, he took note;
Yet stared at nobody, – you stared at him,

And found, less to your pleasure than surprise,
He seemed to know you and expect as much.
So, next time that a neighbour's tongue was loosed,
It marked the shameful and notorious fact,
We had among us, not so much a spy,
As a recording chief-inquisitor,
The town's true master if the town but knew!
We merely kept a governor for form,
While this man walked about and took account
Of all thought, said and acted, then went home,
And wrote it fully to our Lord the King
Who has an itch to know things, he knows why,
And reads them in his bedroom of a night.
Oh, you might smile! there wanted not a touch,
A tang of . . . well, it was not wholly ease
As back into your mind the man's look came.
Stricken in years a little, – such a brow
His eyes had to live under! – clear as flint
On either side the formidable nose
Curved, cut and coloured like an eagle's claw.
Had he to do with A.'s surprising fate?
When altogether old B. disappeared
And young C. got his mistress, – was't our friend,
His letter to the King, that did it all?
What paid the bloodless man for so much pains?
Our Lord the King has favourites manifold,
And shifts his ministry some once a month;
Our city gets new governors at whiles, –
But never word or sign, that I could hear,
Notified to this man about the streets
The King's approval of those letters conned
The last thing duly at the dead of night.
Did the man love his office? Frowned our Lord,
Exhorting when none heard – 'Beseech me not!
Too far above my people, – beneath me!
I set the watch, – how should the people know?
Forget them, keep me all the more in mind!'
Was some such understanding 'twixt the two?

I found no truth in one report at least –
That if you tracked him to his home, down lanes
Beyond the Jewry, and as clean to pace,
You found he ate his supper in a room
Blazing with lights, four Titians on the wall,
And twenty naked girls to change his plate!
Poor man, he lived another kind of life
In that new stuccoed third house by the bridge,
Fresh-painted, rather smart than otherwise!
The whole street might o'erlook him as he sat,
Leg crossing leg, one foot on the dog's back,
Playing a decent cribbage with his maid
(Jacynth, you're sure her name was) o'er the cheese
And fruit, three red halves of starved winter-pears,
Or treat of radishes in April. Nine,
Ten, struck the church clock, straight to bed went he.

My father, like the man of sense he was,
Would point him out to me a dozen times;
''St – 'St,' he'd whisper, 'the Corregidor!'
I had been used to think that personage
Was one with lacquered breeches, lustrous belt,
And feathers like a forest in his hat,
Who blew a trumpet and proclaimed the news,
Announced the bull-fights, gave each church its turn,
And memorized the miracle in vogue!
He had a great observance from us boys;
We were in error; that was not the man.

I'd like now, yet had haply been afraid,
To have just looked, when this man came to die,
And seen who lined the clean gay garret-sides
And stood about the neat low truckle-bed,
With the heavenly manner of relieving guard.
Here had been, mark, the general-in-chief,
Through a whole campaign of the world's life and death,
Doing the King's work all the dim day long,
In his old coat and up to knees in mud,
Smoked like a herring, dining on a crust, –

And, now the day was won, relieved at once!
No further show or need for that old coat,
You are sure, for one thing! Bless us, all the while
How sprucely we are dressed out, you and I!
A second, and the angels alter that.
Well, I could never write a verse, – could you?
Let's to the Prado and make the most of time.

ROBERT BROWNING

Youth and Art

It once might have been, once only:
    We lodged in a street together,
You, a sparrow on the housetop lonely,
    I, a lone she-bird of his feather.

Your trade was with sticks and clay,
    You thumbed, thrust, patted and polished,
Then laughed 'They will see some day
    Smith made, and Gibson demolished.'

My business was song, song, song;
    I chirped, cheeped, trilled and twittered,
'Kate Brown's on the boards ere long,
    And Grisi's existence embittered!'

I earned no more by a warble
    Than you by a sketch in plaster;
You wanted a piece of marble,
    I needed a music-master.

We studied hard in our styles,
    Chipped each at a crust like Hindoos,
For air looked out on the tiles,
    For fun watched each other's windows.

You lounged, like a boy of the South,
    Cap and blouse – nay, a bit of beard too;

Or you got it, rubbing your mouth
    With fingers the clay adhered to.

And I – soon managed to find
    Weak points in the flower-fence facing,
Was forced to put up a blind
    And be safe in my corset-lacing.

No harm! It was not my fault
    If you never turned your eye's tail up
As I shook upon E *in alt*,
    Or ran the chromatic scale up:

For spring bade the sparrows pair,
    And the boys and girls gave guesses,
And stalls in our street looked rare
    With bulrush and watercresses.

Why did you not pinch a flower
    In a pellet of clay and fling it?
Why did not I put a power
    Of thanks in a look, or sing it?

I did look, sharp as a lynx,
    (And yet the memory rankles)
When models arrived, some minx
    Tripped up-stairs, she and her ankles.

But I think I gave you as good!
    'That foreign fellow, – who can know
How she pays, in a playful mood,
    For his tuning her that piano?'

Could you say so, and never say
    'Suppose we join hands and fortunes,
And I fetch her from over the way,
    Her, piano, and long tunes and short tunes?'

No, no: you would not be rash,
    Nor I rasher and something over:
You've to settle yet Gibson's hash,
    And Grisi yet lives in clover.

But you meet the Prince at the Board,
   I'm queen myself at *bals-paré*,
I've married a rich old lord,
   And you're dubbed knight and an RA

Each life unfulfilled, you see;
   It hangs still, patchy and scrappy:
We have not sighed deep, laughed free,
   Starved, feasted, despaired – been happy.

And nobody calls you a dunce,
   And people suppose me clever:
This could but have happened once,
   And we missed it, lost it for ever.

ROBERT BROWNING

'Come down, O maid, from yonder mountain height'

Come down, O maid, from yonder mountain height:
What pleasure lives in height (the shepherd sang)
In height and cold, the splendour of the hills?
But cease to move so near the Heavens, and cease
To glide a sunbeam by the blasted Pine,
To sit a star upon the sparkling spire;
And come, for Love is of the valley, come,
For Love is of the valley, come thou down
And find him; by the happy threshold, he,
Or hand in hand with Plenty in the maize,
Or red with spirted purple of the vats,
Or foxlike in the vine; nor cares to walk
With Death and Morning on the silver horns,
Nor wilt thou snare him in the white ravine,
Nor find him dropt upon the firths of ice,
That huddling slant in furrow-cloven falls
To roll the torrent out of dusky doors:
But follow; let the torrent dance thee down
To find him in the valley; let the wild

Lean-headed Eagles yelp alone, and leave
The monstrous ledges there to slope, and spill
Their thousand wreaths of dangling water-smoke,
That like a broken purpose waste in air:
So waste not thou; but come; for all the vales
Await thee; azure pillars of the hearth
Arise to thee; the children call, and I
Thy shepherd pipe, and sweet is every sound,
Sweeter thy voice, but every sound is sweet;
Myriads of rivulets hurrying thro' the lawn,
The moan of doves in immemorial elms,
And murmuring of innumerable bees.

ALFRED, LORD TENNYSON

'Break, break, break'

Break, break, break,
  On thy cold gray stones, O Sea!
And I would that my tongue could utter
  The thoughts that arise in me.

O well for the fisherman's boy,
  That he shouts with his sister at play!
O well for the sailor lad,
  That he sings in his boat on the bay!

And the stately ships go on
  To their haven under the hill;
But O for the touch of a vanish'd hand,
  And the sound of a voice that is still!

Break, break, break,
  At the foot of thy crags, O Sea!
But the tender grace of a day that is dead
  Will never come back to me.

ALFRED, LORD TENNYSON

The Owl

When cats run home and light is come,
   And dew is cold upon the ground,
And the far-off stream is dumb,
   And the whirring sail goes round,
   And the whirring sail goes round;
     Alone and warming his five wits,
     The white owl in the belfry sits.

When merry milkmaids click the latch,
   And rarely smells the new-mown hay,
And the cock hath sung beneath the thatch
   Twice or thrice his roundelay,
   Twice or thrice his roundelay;
     Alone and warming his five wits,
     The white owl in the belfry sits.

ALFRED, LORD TENNYSON

To E. FitzGerald

Old Fitz, who from your suburb grange,
   Where once I tarried for a while,
Glance at the wheeling Orb of change,
   And greet it with a kindly smile;
Whom yet I see as there you sit
   Beneath your sheltering garden-tree,
And while your doves about you flit,
   And plant on shoulder, hand and knee,
Or on your head their rosy feet,
   As if they knew your diet spares
Whatever moved in that full sheet
   Let down to Peter at his prayers;
Who live on milk and meal and grass;
   And once for ten long weeks I tried
Your table of Pythagoras,

And seem'd at first 'a thing enskied'
(As Shakespeare has it) airy-light
    To float above the ways of men,
Then fell from that half-spiritual height
    Chill'd, till I tasted flesh again
One night when earth was winter-black,
    And all the heavens flash'd in frost;
And on me, half-asleep, came back
    That wholesome heat the blood had lost,
And set me climbing icy capes
    And glaciers, over which there roll'd
To meet me long-arm'd vines with grapes
    Of Eschol hugeness; for the cold
Without, and warmth within me, wrought
    To mould the dream; but none can say
That Lenten fare makes Lenten thought,
    Who reads your golden Eastern lay,
Than which I know no version done
    In English more divinely well;
A planet equal to the sun
    Which cast it, that large infidel
Your Omar; and your Omar drew
    Full-handed plaudits from our best
In modern letters, and from two,
    Old friends outvaluing all the rest,
Two voices heard on earth no more;
    But we old friends are still alive,
And I am nearing seventy-four,
    While you have touch'd at seventy-five,
And so I send a birthday line
    Of greeting; and my son, who dipt
In some forgotten book of mine
    With sallow scraps of manuscript,
And dating many a year ago,
    Has hit on this, which you will take
My Fitz, and welcome, as I know
    Less for its own than for the sake
Of one recalling gracious times,

When, in our younger London days,
You found some merit in my rhymes,
And I more pleasure in your praise.

ALFRED, LORD TENNYSON

Sonnet: Leaves

Leaves of the summer, lovely summer's pride,
  Sweet is the shade below your silent tree,
Whether in waving copses, where ye hide
  My roamings, or in fields that let me see
  The open sky; and whether ye may be
Around the low-stemm'd oak, robust and wide;
Or taper ash upon the mountain side;
  Or lowland elm; your shade is sweet to me.

Whether ye wave above the early flow'rs
  In lively green; or whether, rustling sere,
Ye fly on playful winds, around my feet,

In dying autumn; lovely are your bow'rs,
  Ye early-dying children of the year;
    Holy the silence of your calm retreat.

WILLIAM BARNES

The Eagle

FRAGMENT

He clasps the crag with crooked hands;
Close to the sun in lonely lands,
Ring'd with the azure world, he stands.

The wrinkled sea beneath him crawls;
He watches from his mountain walls,
And like a thunderbolt he falls.

ALFRED, LORD TENNYSON

'Four ducks on a pond'

Four ducks on a pond,
A grass-bank beyond,
A blue sky of spring,
White clouds on the wing;
What a little thing
To remember for years –
To remember with tears!

WILLIAM ALLINGHAM

The Lady of Shalott

PART I

On either side the river lie
Long fields of barley and of rye,
That clothe the wold and meet the sky;
And thro' the field the road runs by
      To many-tower'd Camelot;
And up and down the people go,
Gazing where the lilies blow
Round an island there below,
      The island of Shalott.

Willows whiten, aspens quiver,
Little breezes dusk and shiver
Thro' the wave that runs for ever
By the island in the river
      Flowing down to Camelot.
Four grey walls, and four grey towers,
Overlook a space of flowers,
And the silent isle imbowers
      The Lady of Shalott.

By the margin, willow-veil'd,
Slide the heavy barges trail'd

By slow horses; and unhail'd
The shallop flitteth silken-sail'd
      Skimming down to Camelot:
But who hath seen her wave her hand?
Or at the casement seen her stand?
Or is she known in all the land,
      The Lady of Shalott?

Only reapers, reaping early
In among the bearded barley,
Hear a song that echoes cheerly
From the river winding clearly,
      Down to tower'd Camelot:
And by the moon the reaper weary,
Piling sheaves in uplands airy,
Listening, whispers ''Tis the fairy
      Lady of Shalott.'

PART II

There she weaves by night and day
A magic web with colours gay.
She has heard a whisper say,
A curse is on her if she stay
      To look down to Camelot.
She knows not what the curse may be,
And so she weaveth steadily,
And little other care hath she,
      The Lady of Shalott.

And moving thro' a mirror clear
That hangs before her all the year,
Shadows of the world appear.
There she sees the highway near
      Winding down to Camelot:
There the river eddy whirls,
And there the surly village-churls,
And the red cloaks of market girls,
      Pass onward from Shalott.

Sometimes a troop of damsels glad,
An abbot on an ambling pad,
Sometimes a curly shepherd-lad,
Or long-hair'd page in crimson clad,
      Goes by to tower'd Camelot;
And sometimes thro' the mirror blue
The knights come riding two and two:
She hath no loyal knight and true,
      The Lady of Shalott.

But in her web she still delights
To weave the mirror's magic sights,
For often thro' the silent nights
A funeral, with plumes and lights,
      And music, went to Camelot:
Or when the moon was overhead,
Came two young lovers lately wed;
'I am half sick of shadows,' said
      The Lady of Shalott.

PART III

A bow-shot from her bower-eaves,
He rode between the barley-sheaves,
The sun came dazzling thro' the leaves,
And flamed upon the brazen greaves
      Of bold Sir Lancelot.
A red-cross knight for ever kneel'd
To a lady in his shield,
That sparkled on the yellow field,
      Beside remote Shalott.

The gemmy bridle glitter'd free,
Like to some branch of stars we see
Hung in the golden Galaxy.
The bridle bells rang merrily
      As he rode down to Camelot:
And from his blazon'd baldric slung
A mighty silver bugle hung,

And as he rode his armour rung,
        Beside remote Shalott.

All in the blue unclouded weather
Thick-jewell'd shone the saddle-leather,
The helmet and the helmet-feather
Burn'd like one burning flame together,
        As he rode down to Camelot.
As often thro' the purple night,
Below the starry clusters bright,
Some bearded meteor, trailing light,
        Moves over still Shalott.

His broad clear brow in sunlight glow'd;
On burnish'd hooves his war-horse trode;
From underneath his helmet flow'd
His coal-black curls as on he rode,
        As he rode down to Camelot.
From the bank and from the river
He flash'd into the crystal mirror,
'Tirra lirra,' by the river
        Sang Sir Lancelot.

She left the web, she left the loom,
She made three paces thro' the room,
She saw the water-lily bloom,
She saw the helmet and the plume,
        She look'd down to Camelot.
Out flew the web and floated wide;
The mirror crack'd from side to side;
'The curse is come upon me,' cried
        The Lady of Shalott.

PART IV

In the stormy east-wind straining,
The pale yellow woods were waning,
The broad stream in his banks complaining,
Heavily the low sky raining
        Over tower'd Camelot;

Down she came and found a boat
Beneath a willow left afloat,
And round about the prow she wrote
      The Lady of Shalott.

And down the river's dim expanse –
Like some bold seër in a trance,
Seeing all his own mischance –
With a glassy countenance
      Did she look to Camelot.
And at the closing of the day
She loosed the chain, and down she lay;
The broad stream bore her far away,
      The Lady of Shalott.

Lying, robed in snowy white
That loosely flew to left and right –
The leaves upon her falling light –
Thro' the noises of the night
      She floated down to Camelot:
And as the boat-head wound along
The willowy hills and fields among,
They heard her singing her last song,
      The Lady of Shalott.

Heard a carol, mournful, holy,
Chanted loudly, chanted lowly,
Till her blood was frozen slowly,
And her eyes were darken'd wholly,
      Turn'd to tower'd Camelot.
For ere she reach'd upon the tide
The first house by the water-side,
Singing in her song she died,
      The Lady of Shalott.

Under tower and balcony,
By garden-wall and gallery,
A gleaming shape she floated by,
Dead-pale between the houses high,
      Silent into Camelot.

Out upon the wharfs they came,
Knight and burgher, lord and dame,
And round the prow they read her name,
    The Lady of Shalott.

Who is this? and what is here?
And in the lighted palace near
Died the sound of royal cheer;
And they cross'd themselves for fear,
        All the knights at Camelot:
But Lancelot mused a little space;
He said, 'She has a lovely face;
God in his mercy lend her grace,
        The Lady of Shalott.'

ALFRED, LORD TENNYSON

Song

When I am dead, my dearest,
    Sing no sad songs for me;
Plant thou no roses at my head,
    Nor shady cypress tree:
Be the green grass above me
    With showers and dewdrops wet;
And if thou wilt, remember,
    And if thou wilt, forget.

I shall not see the shadows,
    I shall not feel the rain;
I shall not hear the nightingale
    Sing on, as if in pain:
And dreaming through the twilight
    That doth not rise nor set,
Haply I may remember,
    And haply may forget.

CHRISTINA ROSSETTI

Porphyria's Lover

The rain set early in tonight,
  The sullen wind was soon awake,
It tore the elm-tops down for spite,
  And did its worst to vex the lake:
  I listened with heart fit to break.
When glided in Porphyria; straight
  She shut the cold out and the storm,
And kneeled and made the cheerless grate
  Blaze up, and all the cottage warm;
  Which done, she rose, and from her form
Withdrew the dripping cloak and shawl,
  And laid her soiled gloves by, untied
Her hat and let the damp hair fall,
  And, last, she sat down by my side
  And called me. When no voice replied,
She put my arm about her waist,
  And made her smooth white shoulder bare,
And all her yellow hair displaced,
  And, stooping, made my cheek lie there,
  And spread, o'er all, her yellow hair,
Murmuring how she loved me – she
  Too weak, for all her heart's endeavour,
To set its struggling passion free
  From pride, and vainer ties dissever,
  And give herself to me for ever.
But passion sometimes would prevail,
  Nor could tonight's gay feast restrain
A sudden thought of one so pale
  For love of her, and all in vain:
  So, she was come through wind and rain.
Be sure I looked up at her eyes
  Happy and proud; at last I knew
Porphyria worshipped me; surprise
  Made my heart swell, and still it grew
  While I debated what to do.

43

That moment she was mine, mine, fair,
    Perfectly pure and good: I found
A thing to do, and all her hair
    In one long yellow string I wound
    Three times her little throat around,
And strangled her. No pain felt she;
    I am quite sure she felt no pain.
As a shut bud that holds a bee,
    I warily oped her lids: again
    Laughed the blue eyes without a stain.
And I untightened next the tress
    About her neck; her cheek once more
Blushed bright beneath my burning kiss:
    I propped her head up as before,
    Only, this time my shoulder bore
Her head, which droops upon it still:
    The smiling rosy little head,
So glad it has its utmost will,
    That all it scorned at once is fled,
    And I, its love, am gained instead!
Porphyria's love: she guessed not how
    Her darling one wish would be heard.
And thus we sit together now,
    And all night long we have not stirred,
    And yet God has not said a word!

ROBERT BROWNING

A Birthday

My heart is like a singing bird
    Whose nest is in a watered shoot;
My heart is like an apple tree
    Whose boughs are bent with thickset fruit;
My heart is like a rainbow shell
    That paddles in a halcyon sea;
My heart is gladder than all these
    Because my love is come to me.

Raise me a dais of silk and down;
    Hang it with vair and purple dyes;
Carve it in doves and pomegranates,
    And peacocks with a hundred eyes;
Work it in gold and silver grapes,
    In leaves and silver fleurs-de-lys;
Because the birthday of my life
    Is come, my love is come to me.

CHRISTINA ROSSETTI

'I caught a little ladybird'

I caught a little ladybird
    That flies far away;
I caught a little lady wife
    That is both staid and gay.

Come back, my scarlet ladybird,
    Back from far away;
I weary of my dolly wife,
    My wife that cannot play.

She's such a senseless wooden thing
    She stares the livelong day;
Her wig of gold is stiff and cold
    And cannot change to grey.

CHRISTINA ROSSETTI

London Snow

When men were all asleep the snow came flying,
In large white flakes falling on the city brown,
Stealthily and perpetually settling and loosely lying,
    Hushing the latest traffic of the drowsy town;
Deadening, muffling, stifling its murmurs failing;
Lazily and incessantly floating down and down:
    Silently sifting and veiling road, roof and railing;

Hiding difference, making unevenness even,
Into angles and crevices softly drifting and sailing.
    All night it fell, and when full inches seven
It lay in the depth of its uncompacted lightness,
The clouds blew off from a high and frosty heaven;
    And all woke earlier for the unaccustomed brightness
Of the winter dawning, the strange unheavenly glare:
The eye marvelled – marvelled at the dazzling whiteness;
    The ear hearkened to the stillness of the solemn air;
No sound of wheel rumbling nor of foot falling,
And the busy morning cries came thin and spare.
    Then boys I heard, as they went to school, calling,
They gathered up the crystal manna to freeze
Their tongues with tasting, their hands with snowballing;
    Or rioted in a drift, plunging up to the knees;
Or peering up from under the white-mossed wonder,
'O look at the trees!' they cried, 'O look at the trees!'
    With lessened load a few carts creak and blunder,
Following along the white deserted way,
A country company long dispersed asunder:
    When now already the sun, in pale display
Standing by Paul's high dome, spread forth below
His sparkling beams, and awoke the stir of the day.
    For now doors open, and war is waged with the snow;
And trains of sombre men, past tale of number,
Tread long brown paths, as toward their toil they go:
    But even for them awhile no cares encumber
Their minds diverted; the daily word is unspoken,
The daily thoughts of labour and sorrow slumber
At the sight of the beauty that greets them, for the charm they have
    broken.

ROBERT BRIDGES

The Pied Piper of Hamelin

I

Hamelin Town's in Brunswick,
    By famous Hanover city;
The river Weser, deep and wide,
Washes its wall on the southern side;
A pleasanter spot you never spied;
    But, when begins my ditty,
Almost five hundred years ago,
To see the townsfolk suffer so
    From vermin, was a pity.

II

    Rats!
They fought the dogs and killed the cats,
    And bit the babies in the cradles,
And ate the cheeses out of the vats,
    And licked the soup from the cooks' own ladles,
Split open the kegs of salted sprats,
Made nests inside men's Sunday hats,
And even spoiled the women's chats
    By drowning their speaking
    With shrieking and squeaking
In fifty different sharps and flats.

III

At last the people in a body
    To the Town Hall came flocking:
''Tis clear,' cried they, 'our Mayor's a noddy;
    And as for our Corporation – shocking
To think we buy gowns lined with ermine
For dolts that can't or won't determine
What's best to rid us of our vermin!

47

You hope, because you're old and obese,
To find in the furry civic robe ease?
Rouse up, Sirs! Give your brains a racking
To find the remedy we're lacking,
Or, sure as fate, we'll send you packing!'
At this the Mayor and Corporation
Quaked with a mighty consternation.

IV

An hour they sat in council,
   At length the Mayor broke silence:
'For a guilder I'd my ermine gown sell,
   I wish I were a mile hence!
It's easy to bid one rack one's brain –
I'm sure my poor head aches again,   —
I've scratched it so, and all in vain.
Oh for a trap, a trap, a trap!'
Just as he said this, what should hap
At the chamber door but a gentle tap?
'Bless us,' cried the Mayor, 'what's that?'
(With the Corporation as he sat,
Looking little though wondrous fat;
Nor brighter was his eye, nor moister
Than a too-long-opened oyster,
Save when at noon his paunch grew mutinous
For a plate of turtle green and glutinous)
'Only a scraping of shoes on the mat?
Anything like the sound of a rat
Makes my heart go pit-a-pat!'

V

'Come in!' – the Mayor cried, looking bigger:
And in did come the strangest figure!
His queer long coat from heel to head
Was half of yellow and half of red,
And he himself was tall and thin,
With sharp blue eyes, each like a pin,

And light loose hair, yet swarthy skin,
No tuft on cheek nor beard on chin,
But lips where smiles went out and in;
There was no guessing his kith and kin:
And nobody could enough admire
The tall man and his quaint attire.
Quoth one: 'It's as my great-grandsire,
Starting up at the Trump of Doom's tone,
Had walked this way from his painted tombstone!'

VI

He advanced to the council-table:
And, 'Please your honours,' said he, 'I'm able,
By means of a secret charm, to draw
    All creatures living beneath the sun,
    That creep or swim or fly or run,
After me so as you never saw!
And I chiefly use my charm
On creatures that do people harm,
The mole and toad and newt and viper;
And people call me the Pied Piper.'
(And here they noticed round his neck,
    A scarf of red and yellow stripe,
To match with his coat of the self-same check;
    And at the scarf's end hung a pipe;
And his fingers, they noticed, were ever straying
As if impatient to be playing
Upon this pipe, as low it dangled
Over his vesture so old-fangled.)
'Yet,' said he, 'poor piper as I am,
In Tartary I freed the Cham,
    Last June, from his huge swarms of gnats;
I eased in Asia the Nizam
    Of a monstrous brood of vampire-bats:
And as for what your brain bewilders,
    If I can rid your town of rats
Will you give me a thousand guilders?'

And a moving away of pickle-tub-boards,
And a leaving ajar of conserve-cupboards,
And a drawing the corks of train-oil-flasks,
And a breaking the hoops of butter-casks:
And it seemed as if a voice
   (Sweeter far than by harp or by psaltery
Is breathed) called out, "Oh rats, rejoice!
   The world is grown to one vast drysaltery!
So munch on, crunch on, take your nuncheon,
Breakfast, supper, dinner, luncheon!"
And just as a bulky sugar-puncheon,
All ready staved, like a great sun shone
Glorious scarce an inch before me,
Just as methought it said, "Come, bore me!"
– I found the Weser rolling o'er me.'

VIII

You should have heard the Hamelin people
Ringing the bells till they rocked the steeple.
'Go,' cried the Mayor, 'and get long poles,
Poke out the nests and block up the holes!
Consult with carpenters and builders,
And leave in our town not even a trace
Of the rats!' – when suddenly, up the face
Of the Piper perked in the market-place,
With a, 'First, if you please, my thousand guilders!'

IX

A thousand guilders! The Mayor looked blue;
So did the Corporation too.
For council dinners made rare havoc
With Claret, Moselle, Vin-de-Grave, Hock;
And half the money would replenish
Their cellar's biggest butt with Rhenish.
To pay this sum to a wandering fellow
With a gypsy coat of red and yellow!

Laid his long pipe of smooth straight cane;
And ere he blew three notes (such sweet
Soft notes as yet musician's cunning
Never gave the enraptured air)
There was a rustling that seemed like a bustling
Of merry crowds justling at pitching and hustling,
Small feet were pattering, wooden shoes clattering,
Little hands clapping and little tongues chattering,
And, like fowls in a farm-yard when barley is scattering,
Out came the children running.
All the little boys and girls,
With rosy cheeks and flaxen curls,
And sparkling eyes and teeth like pearls,
Tripping and skipping, ran merrily after
The wonderful music with shouting and laughter.

XIII

The Mayor was dumb, and the Council stood
As if they were changed into blocks of wood.
Unable to move a step, or cry
To the children merrily skipping by,
– Could only follow with the eye
That joyous crowd at the Piper's back.
But how the Major was on the rack,
And the wretched Council's bosoms beat,
As the Piper turned from the High Street
To where the Weser rolled its waters
Right in the way of their sons and daughters!
However he turned from South to West,
And to Koppelberg Hill his steps addressed,
And after him the children pressed;
Great was the joy in every breast.
'He never can cross that mighty top!
He's forced to let the piping drop,
And we shall see our children stop!'
When, lo, as they reached the mountain-side,
A wondrous portal opened wide,

As if a cavern was suddenly hollowed;
And the Piper advanced and the children followed,
And when all were in to the very last,
The door in the mountain-side shut fast.
Did I say, all? No! One was lame,
    And could not dance the whole of the way;
And in after years, if you would blame
    His sadness, he was used to say, —
'It's dull in our town since my playmates left!
I can't forget that I'm bereft
Of all the pleasant sights they see,
Which the Piper also promised me.
For he led us, he said, to a joyous land,
Joining the town and just at hand,
Where waters gushed and fruit-trees grew
And flowers put forth a fairer hue,
And everything was strange and new;
The sparrows were brighter than peacocks here,
And their dogs outran our fallow deer,
And honey-bees had lost their stings,
And horses were born with eagles' wings:
And just as I became assured
My lame foot would be speedily cured,
The music stopped and I stood still,
And found myself outside the hill,
Left alone against my will,
To go now limping as before,
And never hear of the country more!'

XIV

Alas, alas for Hamelin!
    There came into many a burgher's pate
    A text which says that heaven's gate
    Opes to the rich at as easy rate
As the needle's eye takes a camel in!
The mayor sent East, West, North and South,
To offer the Piper, by word of mouth,

Wherever it was men's lot to find him,
Silver and gold to his heart's content,
If he'd only return the way he went,
    And bring the children behind him.
But when they saw 'twas a lost endeavour,
And Piper and dancers were gone for ever,
They made a decree that lawyers never
    Should think their records dated duly
If, after the day of the month and year,
These words did not as well appear
'And so long after what happened here
    On the Twenty-second of July,
Thirteen hundred and seventy-six':
And the better in memory to fix
The place of the children's last retreat,
They called it, the Pied Piper's Street –
Where any one playing on pipe or tabor
Was sure for the future to lose his labour.
Nor suffered they hostelry or tavern
    To shock with mirth a street so solemn;
But opposite the place of the cavern
    They wrote the story on a column,
And on the great church-window painted
The same, to make the world acquainted
How their children were stolen away,
And there it stands to this very day.
And I must not omit to say
That in Transylvania there's a tribe
Of alien people who ascribe
The outlandish ways and dress
On which their neighbours lay such stress,
To their fathers and mothers having risen
Out of some subterraneous prison
Into which they were trepanned
Long time ago in a mighty band
Out of Hamelin town in Brunswick land,
But how or why, they don't understand.

XV

So, Willy, let me and you be wipers
Of scores out with all men – especially pipers!
And, whether they pipe us free frόm rats or frόm mice,
If we've promised them aught, let us keep our promise!

ROBERT BROWNING

A Forsaken Garden

In a coign of the cliff between lowland and highland,
   At the sea-down's edge between windward and lee,
Walled round with rocks as an inland island,
   The ghost of a garden fronts the sea.
A girdle of brushwood and thorn encloses
   The steep square slope of the blossomless bed
Where the weeds that grew green from the graves of its roses
      Now lie dead.

The fields fall southward, abrupt and broken,
   To the low last edge of the long lone land.
If a step should sound or a word be spoken,
   Would a ghost not rise at the strange guest's hand?
So long have the grey bare walks lain guestless,
   Through branches and briars if a man make way,
He shall find no life but the sea-wind's, restless
      Night and day.

The dense hard passage is blind and stifled
   That crawls by a track none turn to climb
To the strait waste place that the years have rifled
   Of all but the thorns that are touched not of time.
The thorns he spares when the rose is taken;
   The rocks are left when he wastes the plain.
The wind that wanders, the weeds wind-shaken,
      These remain.

Not a flower to be pressed of the foot that falls not;
   As the heart of a dead man the seed-plots are dry;

From the thicket of thorns whence the nightingale calls not,
    Could she call, there were never a rose to reply.
Over the meadows that blossom and wither
    Rings but the note of a sea-bird's song;
Only the sun and the rain come hither
        All year long.

The sun burns sere and the rain dishevels
    One gaunt bleak blossom of scentless breath.
Only the wind here hovers and revels
    In a round where life seems barren as death.
Here there was laughing of old, there was weeping,
    Haply, of lovers none ever will know,
Whose eyes went seaward a hundred sleeping
        Years ago.

Heart handfast in heart as they stood, 'Look thither,'
    Did he whisper? 'look forth from the flowers to the sea;
For the foam-flowers endure when the rose-blossoms wither,
    And men that love lightly may die – but we?'
And the same wind sang and the same waves whitened,
    And or ever the garden's last petals were shed,
In the lips that had whispered, the eyes that had lightened,
        Love was dead.

Or they loved their life through, and then went whither?
    And were one to the end – but what end who knows?
Love deep as the sea as a rose must wither,
    As the rose-red seaweed that mocks the rose.
Shall the dead take thought for the dead to love them?
    What love was ever as deep as a grave?
They are loveless now as the grass above them
        Or the wave.

All are at one now, roses and lovers,
    Not known of the cliffs and the fields and the sea.
Not a breath of the time that has been hovers
    In the air now soft with a summer to be.
Not a breath shall there sweeten the seasons hereafter
    Of the flowers or the lovers that laugh now or weep,

When as they that are free now of weeping and laughter
    We shall sleep.

Here death may deal not again for ever;
    Here change may come not till all change end.
From the graves they have made they shall rise up never,
    Who have left nought living to ravage and rend.
Earth, stones, and thorns of the wild ground growing,
    While the sun and the rain live, these shall be;
Till a last wind's breath upon all these blowing
    Roll the sea.

Till the slow sea rise and the sheer cliff crumble,
    Till terrace and meadow the deep gulfs drink,
Till the strength of the waves of the high tides humble
    The fields that lessen, the rocks that shrink,
Here now in his triumph where all things falter,
    Stretched out on the spoils that his own hand spread,
As a god self-slain on his own strange altar,
    Death lies dead.

ALGERNON CHARLES SWINBURNE

'Fair Isle at Sea – thy lovely name'

Fair Isle at Sea – thy lovely name
Soft in my ear like music came.
That sea I loved, and once or twice
I touched at isles of Paradise.

ROBERT LOUIS STEVENSON

By the Sea

Why does the sea moan evermore?
    Shut out from heaven it makes its moan,
It frets against the boundary shore;
    All earth's full rivers cannot fill
    The sea, that drinking thirsteth still.

Sheer miracles of loveliness
   Lie hid in its unlooked-on bed:
Anemones, salt, passionless,
   Blow flower-like; just enough alive
   To blow and multiply and thrive.

Shells quaint with curve, or spot, or spike,
   Encrusted live things argus-eyed,
All fair alike, yet all unlike,
   Are born without a pang, and die
   Without a pang, and so pass by.

CHRISTINA ROSSETTI

The Leper

Nothing is better, I well think,
   Than love; the hidden well-water
Is not so delicate to drink:
   This was well seen of me and her.

I served her in a royal house;
   I served her wine and curious meat.
For will to kiss between her brows,
   I had no heart to sleep or eat.

Mere scorn God knows she had of me,
   A poor scribe, nowise great or fair,
Who plucked his clerk's hood back to see
   Her curled-up lips and amorous hair.

I vex my head with thinking this.
   Yea, though God always hated me,
And hates me now that I can kiss
   Her eyes, plait up her hair to see

How she then wore it on the brows,
   Yet am I glad to have her dead
Here in this wretched wattled house
   Where I can kiss her eyes and head.

Nothing is better, I well know,
　　Than love; no amber in cold sea
Or gathered berries under snow:
　　That is well seen of her and me.

Three thoughts I make my pleasure of:
　　First I take heart and think of this:
That knight's gold hair she chose to love,
　　His mouth she had such will to kiss.

Then I remember that sundawn
　　I brought him by a privy way
Out at her lattice, and thereon
　　What gracious words she found to say.

(Cold rushes for such little feet –
　　Both feet could lie into my hand.
A marvel was it of my sweet
　　Her upright body could so stand.)

'Sweet friend, God give you thank and grace;
　　Now am I clean and whole of shame,
Nor shall men burn me in the face
　　For my sweet fault that scandals them.'

I tell you over word by word.
　　She, sitting edgewise on her bed,
Holding her feet, said thus. The third,
　　A sweeter thing than these, I said.

God, that makes time and ruins it
　　And alters not, abiding God,
Changed with disease her body sweet,
　　The body of love wherein she abode.

Love is more sweet and comelier
　　Than a dove's throat strained out to sing.
All they spat out and cursed at her
　　And cast her forth for a base thing.

They cursed her, seeing how God had wrought
　　This curse to plague her, a curse of his.

Fools were they surely, seeing not
   How sweeter than all sweet she is.

He that had held her by the hair,
   With kissing lips blinding her eyes,
Felt her bright bosom, strained and bare,
   Sigh under him, with short mad cries

Out of her throat and sobbing mouth
   And body broken up with love,
With sweet hot tears his lips were loth
   Her own should taste the savour of,

Yea, he inside whose grasp all night
   Her fervent body leapt or lay,
Stained with sharp kisses red and white,
   Found her a plague to spurn away.

I hid her in this wattled house,
   I served her water and poor bread.
For joy to kiss between her brows
   Time upon time I was nigh dead.

Bread failed; we got but well-water
   And gathered grass with dropping seed.
I had such joy of kissing her,
   I had small care to sleep or feed.

Sometimes when service made me glad
   The sharp tears leapt between my lids,
Falling on her, such joy I had
   To do the service God forbids.

'I pray you let me be at peace,
   Get hence, make room for me to die.'
She said that: her poor lip would cease,
   Put up to mine, and turn to cry.

I said, 'Bethink yourself how love
   Fared in us twain, what either did;
Shall I unclothe my soul thereof?
   That I should do this, God forbid.'

Yea, though God hateth us, he knows
    That hardly in a little thing
Love faileth of the work it does
    Till it grow ripe for gathering.

Six months, and now my sweet is dead
    A trouble takes me; I know not
If all were done well, all well said,
    No word or tender deed forgot.

Too sweet, for the least part in her,
    To have shed life out by fragments; yet,
Could the close mouth catch breath and stir,
    I might see something I forget.

Six months, and I sit still and hold
    In two cold palms her cold two feet.
Her hair, half grey half ruined gold,
    Thrills me and burns me in kissing it.

Love bites and stings me through, to see
    Her keen face made of sunken bones.
Her worn-off eyelids madden me,
    That were shot through with purple once.

She said, 'Be good with me; I grow
    So tired for shame's sake, I shall die
If you say nothing': even so.
    And she is dead now, and shame put by.

Yea, and the scorn she had of me
    In the old time, doubtless vexed her then.
I never should have kissed her. See
    What fools God's anger makes of men!

She might have loved me a little too,
    Had I been humbler for her sake.
But that new shame could make love new
    She saw not – yet her shame did make.

I took too much upon my love,
    Having for such mean service done

Her beauty and all the ways thereof,
  Her face and all the sweet thereon.

Yea, all this while I tended her,
  I know the old love held fast his part:
I know the old scorn waxed heavier,
  Mixed with sad wonder, in her heart.

It may be all my love went wrong –
  A scribe's work writ awry and blurred,
Scrawled after the blind evensong –
  Spoilt music with no perfect word.

But surely I would fain have done
  All things the best I could. Perchance
Because I failed, came short of one,
  She kept at heart that other man's.

I am grown blind with all these things:
  It may be now she hath in sight
Some better knowledge; still there clings
  The old question. Will not God do right?

ALGERNON CHARLES SWINBURNE

'Where lies the land'

Where lies the land to which the ship would go?
Far, far ahead, is all her seamen know.
And where the land she travels from? Away,
Far, far behind, is all that they can say.

On sunny noons upon the deck's smooth face,
Linked arm in arm, how pleasant here to pace;
Or, o'er the stern reclining, watch below
The foaming wake far widening as we go.

On stormy nights when wild north-westers rave,
How proud a thing to fight with wind and wave!
The dripping sailor on the reeling mast
Exults to bear, and scorns to wish it past.

Where lies the land to which the ship would go?
Far, far ahead, is all her seamen know.
And where the land she travels from? Away,
Far, far behind, is all that they can say.

ARTHUR HUGH CLOUGH

Crossing the Bar

Sunset and evening star,
    And one clear call for me!
And may there be no moaning of the bar,
    When I put out to sea,

But such a tide as moving seems asleep,
    Too full for sound and foam,
When that which drew from out the boundless deep
    Turns again home.

Twilight and evening bell,
    And after that the dark!
And may there be no sadness of farewell,
    When I embark;

For tho' from out our bourne of Time and Place
    The flood may bear me far,
I hope to see my Pilot face to face
    When I have crost the bar.

ALFRED, LORD TENNYSON

Dover Beach

The sea is calm to-night.
The tide is full, the moon lies fair
Upon the straits; – on the French coast the light
Gleams and is gone; the cliffs of England stand,
Glimmering and vast, out in the tranquil bay.
Come to the window, sweet is the night-air!

Only, from the long line of spray
Where the sea meets the moon-blanch'd land,
Listen! you hear the grating roar
Of pebbles which the waves draw back, and fling,
At their return, up the high strand,
Begin, and cease, and then again begin,
With tremulous cadence slow, and bring
The eternal note of sadness in.

Sophocles long ago
Heard it on the Ægæan, and it brought
Into his mind the turbid ebb and flow
Of human misery; we
Find also in the sound a thought,
Hearing it by this distant northern sea.

The Sea of Faith
Was once, too, at the full, and round earth's shore
Lay like the folds of a bright girdle furl'd.
But now I only hear
Its melancholy, long, withdrawing roar,
Retreating, to the breath
Of the night-wind, down the vast edges drear
And naked shingles of the world.

Ah, love, let us be true
To one another! for the world, which seems
To lie before us like a land of dreams,
So various, so beautiful, so new,
Hath really neither joy, nor love, nor light,
Nor certitude, nor peace, nor help for pain;
And we are here as on a darkling plain
Swept with confused alarms of struggle and flight,
Where ignorant armies clash by night.

MATTHEW ARNOLD

To Marguerite – Continued

Yes! in the sea of life enisled,
With echoing straits between us thrown,
Dotting the shoreless watery wild,
We mortal millions live *alone*.
The islands feel the enclasping flow,
And then their endless bounds they know.

But when the moon their hollows lights,
And they are swept by balms of spring,
And in their glens, on starry nights,
The nightingales divinely sing;
And lovely notes, from shore to shore
Across the sounds and channels pour –

Oh! then a longing like despair
Is to their farthest caverns sent;
For surely once, they feel, we were
Parts of a single continent!
Now round us spreads the watery plain –
Oh might our marges meet again!

MATTHEW ARNOLD

Magna est veritas

Here, in this little Bay,
Full of tumultuous life and great repose,
Where, twice a day,
The purposeless, glad ocean comes and goes,
Under high cliffs, and far from the huge town,
I sit me down.
For want of me the world's course will not fail:
When all its work is done, the lie shall rot;
The truth is great, and shall prevail,
When none cares whether it prevail or not.

COVENTRY PATMORE

Requiem

Under the wide and starry sky,
Dig the grave and let me lie.
Glad did I live and gladly die,
    And I laid me down with a will.

This be the verse you grave for me:
Here he lies where he longed to be;
Home is the sailor, home from sea,
    And the hunter home from the hill.

ROBERT LOUIS STEVENSON

Dying Speech of an Old Philosopher

I strove with none, for none was worth my strife:
    Nature I loved, and, next to Nature, Art:
I warm'd both hands before the fire of Life;
    It sinks; and I am ready to depart.

WALTER SAVAGE LANDOR

from *The Unknown Eros: A Farewell*

With all my will, but much against my heart,
We two now part.
My Very Dear,
Our solace is, the sad road lies so clear.
It needs no art,
With faint, averted feet
And many a tear,
In our opposed paths to persevere.
Go thou to East, I West.
We will not say
There's any hope, it is so far away.
But, O, my Best,

When the one darling of our widowhead,
The nursling Grief,
Is dead,
And no dews blur our eyes
To see the peach-bloom come in evening skies,
Perchance we may,
Where now this night is day,
And even through faith of still averted feet,
Making full circle of our banishment,
Amazed meet;
The bitter journey to the bourne so sweet
Seasoning the termless feast of our content
With tears of recognition never dry.

COVENTRY PATMORE

from *The Unknown Eros: Departure*

It was not like your great and gracious ways!
Do you, that have nought other to lament,
Never, my Love, repent
Of how, that July afternoon,
You went,
With sudden, unintelligible phrase,
And frighten'd eye,
Upon your journey of so many days,
Without a single kiss, or a good-bye?
I knew, indeed, that you were parting soon;
And so we sate, within the low sun's rays,
You whispering to me, for your voice was weak,
Your harrowing praise.
Well, it was well,
To hear you such things speak,
And I could tell
What made your eyes a growing gloom of love,
As a warm South-wind sombres a March grove.
And it was like your great and gracious ways
To turn your talk on daily things, my Dear,

Lifting the luminous, pathetic lash
To let the laughter flash,
Whilst I drew near,
Because you spoke so low that I could scarcely hear.
But all at once to leave me at the last,
More at the wonder than the loss aghast,
With huddled, unintelligible phrase,
And frighten'd eye,
And go your journey of all days
With not one kiss, or a good-bye,
And the only loveless look the look with which you pass'd:
'Twas all unlike your great and gracious ways.

COVENTRY PATMORE

The Charge of the Light Brigade

I

Half a league, half a league,
  Half a league onward,
All in the valley of Death
  Rode the six hundred.
'Forward, the Light Brigade!
Charge for the guns!' he said;
Into the valley of Death
  Rode the six hundred.

II

'Forward, the Light Brigade!'
Was there a man dismay'd?
Not tho' the soldier knew
  Some one had blunder'd:
Theirs not to make reply,
Theirs not to reason why,
Theirs but to do and die:
Into the valley of Death
  Rode the six hundred.

III

Cannon to right of them,
Cannon to left of them,
Cannon in front of them
  Volley'd and thunder'd;
Storm'd at with shot and shell,
Boldly they rode and well,
  Into the jaws of Death,
  Into the mouth of Hell
    Rode the six hundred.

IV

Flash'd all their sabres bare,
Flash'd as they turn'd in air,
Sabring the gunners there,
Charging an army, while
  All the world wonder'd:
Plunged in the battery-smoke
Right thro' the line they broke;
  Cossack and Russian
Reel'd from the sabre-stroke
  Shatter'd and sunder'd.
Then they rode back, but not,
  Not the six hundred.

V

Cannon to right of them,
Cannon to left of them,
Cannon behind them
  Volley'd and thunder'd;
Storm'd at with shot and shell,
While horse and hero fell,
They that had fought so well
Came thro' the jaws of Death
Back from the mouth of Hell,

All that was left of them,
   Left of six hundred.

VI

When can their glory fade?
O the wild charge they made!
   All the world wonder'd.
Honour the charge they made!
Honour the Light Brigade,
   Noble six hundred!

ALFRED, LORD TENNYSON

Remembrance

Cold in the earth – and the deep snow piled above thee,
Far, far, removed, cold in the dreary grave!
Have I forgot, my only Love, to love thee,
Severed at last by Time's all-wearing wave?

Now, when alone, do my thoughts no longer hover
Over the mountains, on Angora's shore,
Resting their wings where heath and fern-leaves cover
That noble heart for ever, ever more?

Cold in the earth – and fifteen wild Decembers,
From those brown hills, have melted into spring:
Faithful, indeed, is the spirit that remembers
After such years of change and suffering!

Sweet Love of youth, forgive, if I forget thee,
While the world's tide is bearing me along;
Sterner desires and darker hopes beset me,
Hopes which obscure, but cannot do thee wrong!

No later light has lightened up my heaven,
No other star has ever shone for me;
All my life's bliss from thy dear life was given,
All my life's bliss is in the grave with thee.

But, when the days of golden dreams had perished,
And even Despair was powerless to destroy;
Then did I learn how existence could be cherished,
Strengthened, and fed without the aid of joy.

Then did I check the tears of useless passion –
Weaned my young soul from yearning after thine;
Sternly denied its burning wish to hasten
Down to that tomb already more than mine.

And, even yet, I dare not let it languish,
Dare not indulge in memory's rapturous pain;
Once drinking deep of that divinest anguish,
How could I seek the empty world again?

EMILY JANE BRONTË

Remember

Remember me when I am gone away,
   Gone far away into the silent land;
   When you can no more hold me by the hand,
Nor I half turn to go yet turning stay.
Remember me when no more day by day
   You tell me of our future that you planned:
   Only remember me; you understand
It will be late to counsel then or pray.
Yet if you should forget me for a while
   And afterwards remember, do not grieve:
   For if the darkness and corruption leave
   A vestige of the thoughts that once I had,
Better by far you should forget and smile
   Than that you should remember and be sad.

CHRISTINA ROSSETTI

The Toys

My little Son, who look'd from thoughtful eyes
And moved and spoke in quiet grown-up wise,
Having my law the seventh time disobey'd,
I struck him, and dismiss'd
With hard words and unkiss'd,
His Mother, who was patient, being dead.
Then, fearing lest his grief should hinder sleep,
I visited his bed,
But found him slumbering deep,
With darken'd eyelids, and their lashes yet
From his late sobbing wet.
And I, with moan,
Kissing away his tears, left others of my own;
For, on a table drawn beside his head,
He had put, within his reach,
A box of counters and a red–vein'd stone,
A piece of glass abraded by the beach
And six or seven shells,
A bottle with bluebells
And two French copper coins, ranged there with careful art,
To comfort his sad heart.
So when that night I pray'd
To God, I wept, and said:
Ah, when at last we lie with tranced breath,
Not vexing Thee in death,
And Thou rememberest of what toys
We made our joys,
How weakly understood,
Thy great commanded good,
Then, fatherly not less
Than I whom Thou hast moulded from the clay,
Thou'lt leave Thy wrath, and say,
'I will be sorry for their childishness.'

COVENTRY PATMORE

'Long neglect has worn away'

Long neglect has worn away
Half the sweet enchanting smile;
Time has turned the bloom to grey;
Mould and damp the face defile.

But that lock of silky hair,
Still beneath the picture twined,
Tells what once those features were,
Paints their image on the mind.

Fair the hand that traced that line,
'Dearest, ever deem me true';
Swiftly flew the fingers fine
When the pen that motto drew.

EMILY JANE BRONTË

Love and Friendship

Love is like the wild rose briar,
Friendship, like the holly tree
The holly is dark when the rose briar blooms,
But which will bloom most constantly?

The wild rose briar is sweet in spring,
Its summer blossoms scent the air
Yet wait till winter comes again
And who will call the wild-briar fair?

Then scorn the silly rose-wreath now
And deck thee with the holly's sheen
That when December blights thy brow
He still may leave thy garland green –

EMILY JANE BRONTË

from *Modern Love*

By this he knew she wept with waking eyes:
That, at his hand's light quiver by her head,
The strange low sobs that shook their common bed,
Were called into her with a sharp surprise,
And strangled mute, like little gaping snakes,
Dreadfully venomous to him. She lay
Stone-still, and the long darkness flowed away
With muffled pulses. Then, as midnight makes
Her giant heart of Memory and Tears
Drink the pale drug of silence, and so beat
Sleep's heavy measure, they from head to feet
Were moveless, looking through their dead black years,
By vain regret scrawled over the blank wall.
Like sculptured effigies they might be seen
Upon their marriage-tomb, the sword between;
Each wishing for the sword that severs all.

GEORGE MEREDITH

'Say not the struggle nought availeth'

Say not the struggle nought availeth,
   The labour and the wounds are vain,
The enemy faints not, nor faileth,
   And as things have been, things remain.

If hopes were dupes, fears may be liars;
   It may be, in yon smoke concealed,
Your comrades chase e'en now the fliers,
   And, but for you, possess the field.

For while the tired waves, vainly breaking,
   Seem here no painful inch to gain,
Far back through creeks and inlets making
   Came, silent, flooding in, the main,

And not by eastern windows only,
   When daylight comes, comes in the light,
In front the sun climbs slow, how slowly,
   But westward, look, the land is bright.

ARTHUR HUGH CLOUGH

The Forced Recruit

SOLFERINO 1859

In the ranks of the Austrian you found him,
   He died with his face to you all;
Yet bury him here where around him
   You honor your bravest that fall.

Venetian, fair-featured and slender,
   He lies shot to death in his youth,
With a smile on his lips over-tender
   For any mere soldier's dead mouth.

No stranger, and yet not a traitor,
   Though alien the cloth on his breast,
Underneath it how seldom a greater
   Young heart has a shot sent to rest!

By your enemy tortured and goaded
   To march with them, stand in their file,
His musket (see) never was loaded,
   He facing your guns with that smile!

As orphans yearn on to their mothers,
   He yearned to your patriot bands; –
'Let me die for our Italy, brothers,
   If not in your ranks, by your hands!

'Aim straightly, fire steadily! spare me
   A ball in the body which may
Deliver my heart here, and tear me
   This badge of the Austrian away!'

So thought he, so died he this morning.
　　What then? many others have died.
Ay, but easy for men to die scorning
　　The death-stroke, who fought side by side –

One tricolor floating above them;
　　Struck down 'mid triumphant acclaims
Of an Italy rescued to love them
　　And blazon the brass with their names.

But he, – without witness or honour,
　　Mixed, shamed in his country's regard,
With the tyrants who march in upon her,
　　Died faithful and passive: 't was hard.

'T was sublime. In a cruel restriction
　　Cut off from the guerdon of sons,
With most filial obedience, conviction,
　　His soul kissed the lips of her guns.

That moves you? Nay, grudge not to show it,
　　While digging a grave for him here:
The others who died, says your poet,
　　Have glory, – let *him* have a tear.

ELIZABETH BARRETT BROWNING

The Woodspurge

The wind flapped loose, the wind was still,
Shaken out dead from tree and hill:
I had walked on at the wind's will, –
I sat now, for the wind was still.

Between my knees my forehead was, –
My lips drawn in, said not Alas!
My hair was over in the grass,
My naked ears heard the day pass.

My eyes, wide open, had the run
Of some ten weeds to fix upon;

77

Among those few, out of the sun,
The woodspurge flowered, three cups in one.

From perfect grief there need not be
Wisdom or even memory:
One thing then learnt remains to me, –
The woodspurge has a cup of three.

DANTE GABRIEL ROSSETTI

The Latest Decalogue

Thou shalt have one God only; who
Would be at the expense of two?
No graven images may be
Worshipped, except the currency:
Swear not at all; for for thy curse
Thine enemy is none the worse:
At church on Sunday to attend
Will serve to keep the world thy friend:
Honour thy parents; that is, all
From whom advancement may befall:
Thou shalt not kill; but needst not strive
Officiously to keep alive:

Do not adultery commit;
Advantage rarely comes of it:
Thou shalt not steal; an empty feat,
When it's so lucrative to cheat:
Bear not false witness; let the lie
Have time on its own wings to fly:
Thou shalt not covet; but tradition
Approves all forms of competition.

The sum of all is, thou shalt love,
If any body, God above:
At any rate shalt never labour
More than thyself to love thy neighbour.

ARTHUR HUGH CLOUGH

'"There is no God," the wicked saith'

'There is no God,' the wicked saith,
  'And truly it's a blessing,
For what he might have done with us
  It's better only guessing.'

'There is no God,' a youngster thinks,
  'Or really, if there may be,
He surely didn't mean a man
  Always to be a baby.'

'There is no God, or if there is,'
  The tradesman thinks, ''twere funny
If he should take it ill in me
  To make a little money.'

'Whether there be,' the rich man says,
  'It matters very little,
For I and mine, thank somebody,
  Are not in want of victual.'

Some others, also, to themselves
  Who scarce so much as doubt it,
Think there is none, when they are well,
  And do not think about it.

But country folks who live beneath
  The shadow of the steeple;
The parson and the parson's wife,
  And mostly married people;

Youths green and happy in first love,
  So thankful for illusion;
And men caught out in what the world
  Calls guilt, in first confusion;

And almost every one when age,
  Disease, or sorrows strike him,

Inclines to think there is a God,
Or something very like Him.

ARTHUR HUGH CLOUGH

''Tis Christmas weather'

'Tis Christmas weather, and a country house
Receives us: rooms are full: we can but get
An attic-crib. Such lovers will not fret
At that, it is half-said. The great carouse
Knocks hard upon the midnight's hollow door,
But when I knock at hers, I see the pit.
Why did I come here in that dullard fit?
I enter, and lie couched upon the floor.
Passing, I caught the coverlet's quick beat: –
Come, Shame, burn to my soul! and Pride, and Pain –
Foul demons that have tortured me, enchain!
Out in the freezing darkness the lambs bleat.
The small bird stiffens in the low starlight.
I know not how, but shuddering as I slept,
I dreamed a banished angel to me crept:
My feet were nourished on her breasts all night.

GEORGE MEREDITH

'At dinner, she is hostess, I am host'

At dinner, she is hostess, I am host.
Went the feast ever cheerfuller? She keeps
The Topic over intellectual deeps
In buoyancy afloat. They see no ghost.
With sparkling surface-eyes we ply the ball:
It is in truth a most contagious game:
HIDING THE SKELETON, shall be its name.
Such play as this, the devils might appal!
But here's the greater wonder; in that we
Enamoured of an acting nought can tire,

Each other, like true hypocrites, admire;
Warm-lighted looks, Love's ephemerioe,
Shoot gaily o'er the dishes and the wine.
We waken envy of our happy lot.
Fast, sweet, and golden, shows the marriage-knot.
Dear guests, you now have seen Love's corpse-light shine.

GEORGE MEREDITH

'In Autumn when the woods are red'

In Autumn when the woods are red
And skies are grey and clear,
The sportsmen seek the wild fowls' bed
Or follow down the deer;
And Cupid hunts by haugh and head,
By riverside and mere,
I walk, not seeing where I tread
And keep my heart with fear,
Sir, have an eye, on where you tread,
And keep your heart with fear,
For something lingers here;
A touch of April not yet dead,
In Autumn when the woods are red
And skies are grey and clear.

ROBERT LOUIS STEVENSON

'Last night we had a thunderstorm'

Last night we had a thunderstorm in style.
The wild lightning streaked the airs,
As though my God fell down a pair of stairs.
The thunder boomed and bounded all the while;
All cried and sat by water-side and stile –
To mop our brow had been our chief of cares.
I lay in bed with a Voltairean smile,
The terror of good, simple guilty pairs,

And made this rondeau in ironic style,
Last night we had a thunderstorm in style.
Our God the Father fell down-stairs,
The stark blue lightning went its flight, the while,
The very rain you might have heard a mile –
The strenuous faithful buckled to their prayers.

ROBERT LOUIS STEVENSON

A Toccata of Galuppi's

Oh Galuppi, Baldassaro, this is very sad to find!
I can hardly misconceive you; it would prove me deaf and blind;
But although I take your meaning, 't is with such a heavy mind!

Here you come with your old music, and here's all the good it brings.
What, they lived once thus at Venice where the merchants were the
    kings,
Where Saint Mark's is, where the Doges used to wed the sea with
    rings?

Ay, because the sea's the street there; and 't is arched by . . . what you
    call
. . . Shylock's bridge with houses on it, where they kept the carnival:
I was never out of England – it's as if I saw it all.

Did young people take their pleasure when the sea was warm in May?
Balls and masks begun at midnight, burning ever to midday,
When they made up fresh adventures for the morrow, do you say?

Was a lady such a lady, cheeks so round and lips so red, –
On her neck the small face buoyant, like a bell-flower on its bed,
O'er the breast's superb abundance where a man might base his head?

Well, and it was graceful of them – they'd break talk off and afford
– She, to bite her mask's black velvet – he, to finger on his sword,
While you sat and played Toccatas, stately at the clavichord?

What? Those lesser thirds so plaintive, sixths diminished, sigh on
    sigh,

Told them something? Those suspensions, those solutions – 'Must we
    die?'
Those commiserating sevenths – 'Life might last! we can but try!'

'Were you happy?' – 'Yes' – 'And are you still as happy?' – 'Yes. And
    you?'
– 'Then, more kisses!' – 'Did *I* stop them, when a million seemed so
    few?'
Hark, the dominant's persistence till it must be answered to!

So, an octave struck the answer. Oh, they praised you, I dare say!
'Brave Galuppi! that was music! good alike at grave and gay!
I can always leave off talking when I hear a master play!'

Then they left you for their pleasure: till in due time, one by one,
Some with lives that came to nothing, some with deeds as well
    undone,
Death stepped tacitly and took them where they never see the sun.

But when I sit down to reason, think to take my stand nor swerve,
While I triumph o'er a secret wrung from nature's close reserve,
In you come with your cold music till I creep thro' every nerve.

Yes, you, like a ghostly cricket, creaking where a house was burned:
'Dust and ashes, dead and done with, Venice spent what Venice
    earned.
The soul, doubtless, is immortal – where a soul can be discerned.

'Yours for instance: you know physics, something of geology,
Mathematics are your pastime; souls shall rise in their degree;
Butterflies may dread extinction, – you'll not die, it cannot be!

'As for Venice and her people, merely born to bloom and drop,
Here on earth they bore their fruitage, mirth and folly were the crop:
What of soul was left, I wonder, when the kissing had to stop?

'Dust and ashes!' So you creak it, and I want the heart to scold.
Dear dead women, with such hair, too – what's become of all the gold
Used to hang and brush their bosoms? I feel chilly and grown old.

ROBERT BROWNING

'I wake and feel the fell of dark'

I wake and feel the fell of dark, not day.
What hours, O what black hoürs we have spent
This night! what sights you, heart, saw; ways you went!
And more must, in yet longer light's delay.

With witness I speak this. But where I say
Hours I mean years, mean life. And my lament
Is cries countless, cries like dead letters sent
To dearest him that lives alas! away.

I am gall, I am heartburn. God's most deep decree
Bitter would have me taste: my taste was me;
Bones built in me, flesh filled, blood brimmed the curse.

Selfyeast of spirit a dull dough sours. I see
The lost are like this, and their scourge to be
As I am mine, their sweating selves; but worse.

GERARD MANLEY HOPKINS

Inversnaid

This darksome burn, horseback brown,
His rollrock highroad roaring down,
In coop and in comb the fleece of his foam
Flutes and low to the lake falls home.

A windpuff-bonnet of fáwn-fróth
Turns and twindles over the broth
Of a pool so pitchblack, féll-frówning,
It rounds and rounds Despair to drowning.

Degged with dew, dappled with dew
Are the groins of the braes that the brook treads through,
Wiry heathpacks, flitches of fern,
And the beadbonny ash that sits over the burn.

What would the world be, once bereft
Of wet and of wilderness? Let them be left,
O let them be left, wildness and wet;
Long live the weeds and the wilderness yet.

GERARD MANLEY HOPKINS

Pied Beauty

Glory be to God for dappled things –
   For skies of couple-colour as a brinded cow;
     For rose-moles all in stipple upon trout that swim;
Fresh-firecoal chestnut-falls; finches' wings;
   Landscape plotted and pieced – fold, fallow, and plough;
     And áll trádes, their gear and tackle and trim.

All things counter, original, spare, strange;
   Whatever is fickle, freckled (who knows how?)
     With swift, slow; sweet, sour; adazzle, dim;
He fathers-forth whose beauty is past change:
          Praise him.

GERARD MANLEY HOPKINS

God's Grandeur

The world is charged with the grandeur of God.
   It will flame out, like shining from shook foil;
   It gathers to a greatness, like the ooze of oil
Crushed. Why do men then now not reck his rod?
Generations have trod, have trod, have trod;
   And all is seared with trade; bleared, smeared with toil;
   And wears man's smudge and shares man's smell: the soil
Is bare now, nor can foot feel, being shod.

And for all this, nature is never spent;
   There lives the dearest freshness deep down things;
And though the last lights off the black West went
   Oh, morning, at the brown brink eastwards, springs –

Because the Holy Ghost over the bent
   World broods with warm breast and with ah! bright wings.

GERARD MANLEY HOPKINS

Binsey Poplars

FELLED 1879

My aspens dear, whose airy cages quelled,
Quelled or quenched in leaves the leaping sun,
All felled, felled, are all felled;
   Of a fresh and following folded rank
            Not spared, not one
            That dandled a sandalled
         Shadow that swam or sank
On meadow and river and wind-wandering weed-winding bank.

O if we but knew what we do
         When we delve or hew –
   Hack and rack the growing green!
         Since country is so tender
   To touch, her being só slender,
   That, like this sleek and seeing ball
   But a prick will make no eye at all,
   Where we, even where we mean

            To mend her we end her,
         When we hew or delve:
After-comers cannot guess the beauty been.
   Ten or twelve, only ten or twelve
      Strokes of havoc únselve
         The sweet especial scene,
      Rural scene, a rural scene,
Sweet especial rural scene.

GERARD MANLEY HOPKINS

Spring

Nothing is so beautiful as Spring –
  When weeds, in wheels, shoot long and lovely and lush;
  Thrush's eggs look little low heavens, and thrush
Through the echoing timber does so rinse and wring
The ear, it strikes like lightnings to hear him sing;
  The glassy peartree leaves and blooms, they brush
  The descending blue; that blue is all in a rush
With richness; the racing lambs too have fair their fling.

What is all this juice and all this joy?
  A strain of the earth's sweet being in the beginning
In Eden garden. – Have, get, before it cloy,
  Before it cloud, Christ, lord, and sour with sinning,
Innocent mind and Mayday in girl and boy,
  Most, O maid's child, thy choice and worthy the winning.

GERARD MANLEY HOPKINS

A Winter Night

It was a chilly winter's night;
  And frost was glitt'ring on the ground,
And evening stars were twinkling bright;
  And from the gloomy plain around
    Came no sound,
But where, within the wood-girt tow'r,
The churchbell slowly struck the hour;
As if that all of human birth
  Had risen to the final day,
And soaring from the wornout earth
  Were called in hurry and dismay,
    Far away;
And I alone of all mankind
Were left in loneliness behind.

WILLIAM BARNES

A Crocodile

Hard by the lilied Nile I saw
A duskish river-dragon stretched along,
The brown habergeon of his limbs enamelled
With sanguine almandines and rainy pearl:
And on his back there lay a young one sleeping,
No bigger than a mouse; with eyes like beads,
And a small fragment of its speckled egg
Remaining on its harmless, pulpy snout;
A thing to laugh at, as it gaped to catch
The baulking merry flies. In the iron jaws
Of the great devil-beast, like a pale soul
Fluttering in rocky hell, lightsomely flew
A snowy trochilus, with roseate beak
Tearing the hairy leeches from his throat.

THOMAS LOVELL BEDDOES

'How doth the little crocodile'

How doth the little crocodile
    Improve his shining tail,
And pour the waters of the Nile
    On every golden scale!

How cheerfully he seems to grin,
    How neatly spreads his claws,
And welcomes little fishes in,
    With gently smiling jaws!

LEWIS CARROLL

'In winter, when the fields are white'

In winter, when the fields are white,
I sing this song for your delight –

In spring, when woods are getting green,
I'll try and tell you what I mean:

In summer, when the days are long,
Perhaps you'll understand the song:

In autumn, when the leaves are brown,
Take pen and ink, and write it down.

I sent a message to the fish:
I told them 'This is what I wish.'

The little fishes of the sea,
They sent an answer back to me.

The little fishes' answer was
'We cannot do it, Sir, because –'

I sent to them again to say
'It will be better to obey.'

The fishes answered, with a grin,
'Why, what a temper you are in!'

I told them once, I told them twice:
They would not listen to advice.

I took a kettle large and new,
Fit for the deed I had to do.

My heart went hop, my heart went thump:
I filled the kettle at the pump.

Then some one came to me and said
'The little fishes are in bed.'

I said to him, I said it plain,
'Then you must wake them up again.'

I said it very loud and clear:
I went and shouted in his ear.

But he was very stiff and proud:
He said, 'You needn't shout so loud!'

And he was very proud and stiff:
He said 'I'd go and wake them, if –'

I took a corkscrew from the shelf:
I went to wake them up myself.

And when I found the door was locked,
I pulled and pushed and kicked and knocked.

And when I found the door was shut,
I tried to turn the handle, but –

LEWIS CARROLL

The Jumblies

They went to sea in a Sieve, they did,
   In a Sieve they went to sea:
In spite of all their friends could say,
On a winter's morn, on a stormy day,
   In a Sieve they went to sea!
And when the Sieve turned round and round,
And every one cried, 'You'll all be drowned!'
They called aloud, 'Our Sieve ain't big,
But we don't care a button! we don't care a fig!
   In a Sieve we'll go to sea!'
     Far and few, far and few,
       Are the lands where the Jumblies live;
       Their heads are green, and their hands are blue,
       And they went to sea in a Sieve.

They sailed away in a Sieve, they did,
   In a Sieve they sailed so fast,
With only a beautiful pea-green veil
Tied with a riband by way of a sail,
   To a small tobacco-pipe mast;
And every one said, who saw them go,
'O won't they be soon upset, you know!
For the sky is dark, and the voyage is long,
And happen what may, it's extremely wrong

In a Sieve to sail so fast!'
    Far and few, far and few,
        Are the lands where the Jumblies live;
        Their heads are green, and their hands are blue,
        And they went to sea in a Sieve.

The water it soon came in, it did,
    The water it soon came in;
So to keep them dry, they wrapped their feet
In a pinky paper all folded neat,
    And they fastened it down with a pin.
And they passed the night in a crockery-jar,
And each of them said, 'How wise we are!
Though the sky be dark, and the voyage be long,
Yet we never can think we were rash or wrong,
    While round in our Sieve we spin!'
        Far and few, far and few,
            Are the lands where the Jumblies live;
            Their heads are green, and their hands are blue,
            And they went to sea in a Sieve.

And all night long they sailed away;
    And when the sun went down,
They whistled and warbled a moony song
To the echoing sound of a coppery gong,
    In the shade of the mountains brown.
'O Timballoo! How happy we are,
When we live in a Sieve and a crockery-jar,
And all night long in the moonlight pale,
We sail away with a pea-green sail,
    In the shade of the mountains brown!'
        Far and few, far and few,
            Are the lands where the Jumblies live;
            Their heads are green, and their hands are blue,
            And they went to sea in a Sieve.

They sailed to the Western Sea, they did,
    To a land all covered with trees,
And they bought an Owl, and a useful Cart,
And a pound of Rice, and a Cranberry Tart,

And a hive of silvery Bees.
And they bought a Pig, and some green Jack-daws,
And a lovely Monkey with lollipop paws,
And forty bottles of Ring-Bo-Ree,
    And no end of Stilton Cheese.
        Far and few, far and few,
            Are the lands where the Jumblies live;
            Their heads are green, and their hands are blue,
            And they went to sea in a Sieve.

And in twenty years they all came back,
    In twenty years or more,
And every one said, 'How tall they've grown!
For they've been to the Lakes, and the Torrible Zone,
    And the hills of the Chankly Bore';
And they drank their health, and gave them a feast
Of dumplings made of beautiful yeast;
And every one said, 'If we only live,
We too will go to sea in a Sieve, –
    To the hills of the Chankly Bore!'
        Far and few, far and few,
            Are the lands where the Jumblies live;
            Their heads are green, and their hands are blue,
            And they went to sea in a Sieve.

EDWARD LEAR

'How pleasant to know Mr Lear!'

'How pleasant to know Mr Lear!'
    Who has written such volumes of stuff!
Some think him ill-tempered and queer,
    But a few think him pleasant enough.

His mind is concrete and fastidious,
    His nose is remarkably big;
His visage is more or less hideous,
    His beard it resembles a wig.

He has ears, and two eyes, and ten fingers,
    Leastways if you reckon two thumbs;
Long ago he was one of the singers,
    But now he is one of the dumbs.

He sits in a beautiful parlour,
    With hundreds of books on the wall;
He drinks a great deal of Marsala,
    But never gets tipsy at all.

He has many friends, laymen and clerical,
    Old Foss is the name of his cat:
His body is perfectly spherical,
    He weareth a runcible hat.

When he walks in a waterproof white,
    The children run after him so!
Calling out, 'He's come out in his night-
    gown, that crazy old Englishman, oh!'

He weeps by the side of the ocean,
    He weeps on the top of the hill;
He purchases pancakes and lotion,
    And chocolate shrimps from the mill.

He reads but he cannot speak Spanish,
    He cannot abide ginger-beer:
Ere the days of his pilgrimage vanish,
    How pleasant to know Mr Lear!

EDWARD LEAR

from *Sylvie and Bruno*

'He thought he saw an Elephant,
    That practised on a fife:
He looked again, and found it was
    A letter from his wife.
"At length I realize," he said,
    "The bitterness of Life!"'

'He thought he saw a Buffalo
  Upon the chimney-piece:
He looked again, and found it was
  His Sister's Husband's Niece.
"Unless you leave this house," he said,
  "I'll send for the Police!"'

'He thought he saw a Banker's Clerk
  Descending from the bus:
He looked again, and found it was
  A Hippopotamus:
"If this should stay to dine," he said,
  "There won't be much for us!"'

'He thought he saw a Kangaroo
  That worked a coffee-mill:
He looked again, and found it was
  A Vegetable-pill.
"Were I to swallow this," he said,
  "I should be very ill!"'

'He thought he saw a Coach-and-four
  That stood beside his bed:
He looked again, and found it was
  A Bear without a Head.
"Poor thing," he said, "poor silly thing!
  It's waiting to be fed!"'

'He thought he saw an Albatross
  That fluttered round the lamp:
He looked again, and found it was
  A Penny-postage stamp.
"You'd best be getting home," he said:
  "The nights are very damp!"'

'He thought he saw a Garden Door
  That opened with a key:
He looked again, and found it was
  A Double Rule of Three:
"And all its mystery," he said,
  "Is clear as day to me!"'

'He thought he saw an Argument
        That proved he was the Pope:
He looked again, and found it was
        A Bar of Mottled Soap.
"A fact so dread," he faintly said,
        "Extinguishes all hope!"'

LEWIS CARROLL

'You are old, Father William'

'You are old, Father William,' the young man said,
    'And your hair has become very white;
And yet you incessantly stand on your head –
    Do you think, at your age, it is right?'

'In my youth,' Father William replied to his son,
    'I feared it might injure the brain;
But, now that I'm perfectly sure I have none,
    Why, I do it again and again.'

'You are old,' said the youth, 'as I mentioned before,
    And have grown most uncommonly fat;
Yet you turned a back-somersault in at the door –
    Pray, what is the reason of that?'

'In my youth,' said the sage, as he shook his grey locks,
    'I kept all my limbs very supple
By the use of this ointment – one shilling the box –
    Allow me to sell you a couple?'

'You are old,' said the youth, 'and your jaws are too weak
    For anything tougher than suet;
Yet you finished the goose, with the bones and the beak –
    Pray, how did you manage to do it?'

'In my youth,' said his father, 'I took to the law,
    And argued each case with my wife;
And the muscular strength, which it gave to my jaw,
    Has lasted the rest of my life.'

'You are old,' said the youth, 'one would hardly suppose
    That your eye was as steady as ever;
Yet you balanced an eel on the end of your nose –
    What made you so awfully clever?'

'I have answered three questions, and that is enough,'
    Said his father, 'Don't give yourself airs!
Do you think I can listen all day to such stuff?
    Be off, or I'll kick you down-stairs!'

LEWIS CARROLL

J. S. Mill

John Stuart Mill,
By a mighty effort of will,
Overcame his natural bonhomie
And wrote 'Principles of Political Economy'.

EDMUND CLERIHEW BENTLEY

Lord Clive

What I like about Clive
Is that he is no longer alive.
There is a great deal to be said
For being dead.

EDMUND CLERIHEW BENTLEY

George III

George the Third
Ought never to have occurred.
One can only wonder
At so grotesque a blunder.

EDMUND CLERIHEW BENTLEY

Savonarola

Savonarola
Declined to wear a bowler,
Expressing the view that it was gammon
To talk of serving God and Mammon.

EDMUND CLERIHEW BENTLEY

The Hunting of the Snark

FIT THE FIRST

The Landing

'Just the place for a Snark!' the Bellman cried,
  As he landed his crew with care;
Supporting each man on the top of the tide
  By a finger entwined in his hair.

'Just the place for a Snark! I have said it twice:
  That alone should encourage the crew.
Just the place for a Snark! I have said it thrice:
  What I tell you three times is true.'

The crew was complete: it included a Boots –
  A maker of Bonnets and Hoods –
A Barrister, brought to arrange their disputes –
  And a Broker, to value their goods.

A Billiard-marker, whose skill was immense,
  Might perhaps have won more than his share –
But a Banker, engaged at enormous expense,
  Had the whole of their cash in his care.

There was also a Beaver, that paced on the deck,
  Or would sit making lace in the bow:
And had often (the Bellman said) saved them from wreck
  Though none of the sailors knew how.

There was one who was famed for the number of things
　　He forgot when he entered the ship:
His umbrella, his watch, all his jewels and rings,
　　And the clothes he had bought for the trip.

He had forty-two boxes, all carefully packed,
　　With his name painted clearly on each:
But, since he omitted to mention the fact,
　　They were all left behind on the beach.

The loss of his clothes hardly mattered, because
　　He had seven coats on when he came,
With three pair of boots – but the worst of it was,
　　He had wholly forgotten his name.

He would answer to 'Hi' or to any loud cry,
　　Such as 'Fry me!' or 'Fritter my wig!'
To 'What-you-may-call-um!' or 'What-was-his-name!'
　　But especially 'Thing-um-a-jig!'

While, for those who preferred a more forcible word,
　　He had different names from these:
His intimate friends called him 'Candle-ends',
　　And his enemies 'Toasted-cheese'.

'His form is ungainly – his intellect small –'
　　(So the Bellman would often remark) –
'But his courage is perfect! And that, after all,
　　Is the thing that one needs with a Snark.'

He would joke with hyænas, returning their stare
　　With an impudent wag of the head:
And he once went a walk, paw-in-paw, with a bear,
　　'Just to keep up its spirits,' he said.

He came as a Baker: but owned, when too late –
　　And it drove the poor Bellman half-mad –
He could only bake Bridecake – for which, I may state,
　　No materials were to be had.

The last of the crew needs especial remark,
  Though he looked an incredible dunce:
He had just one idea – but, that one being 'Snark',
  The good Bellman engaged him at once.

He came as a Butcher: but gravely declared,
  When the ship had been sailing a week,
He could only kill Beavers. The Bellman looked scared,
  And was almost too frightened to speak:

But at length he explained, in a tremulous tone,
  There was only one Beaver on board;
And that was a tame one he had of his own,
  Whose death would be deeply deplored.

The Beaver, who happened to hear the remark,
  Protested, with tears in its eyes,
That not even the rapture of hunting the Snark
  Could atone for that dismal surprise!

It strongly advised that the Butcher should be
  Conveyed in a separate ship:
But the Bellman declared that would never agree
  With the plans he had made for the trip:

Navigation was always a difficult art,
  Though with only one ship and one bell:
And he feared he must really decline, for his part,
  Undertaking another as well.

The Beaver's best course was, no doubt, to procure
  A second-hand dagger-proof coat –
So the Baker advised it – and next, to insure
  Its life in some Office of note:

This the Baker suggested, and offered for hire
  (On moderate terms), or for sale,
Two excellent Policies, one Against Fire
  And one Against Damage From Hail.

Yet still, ever after that sorrowful day,
  Whenever the Butcher was by,

The Beaver kept looking the opposite way,
    And appeared unaccountably shy.

FIT THE SECOND

The Bellman's Speech

The Bellman himself they all praised to the skies –
    Such a carriage, such ease and such grace!
Such solemnity, too! One could see he was wise,
    The moment one looked in his face!

He had bought a large map representing the sea,
    Without the least vestige of land:
And the crew were much pleased when they found it to be
    A map they could all understand.

'What's the good of Mercator's North Poles and Equators,
    Tropics, Zones, and Meridian Lines?'
So the Bellman would cry: and the crew would reply
    'They are merely conventional signs!

'Other maps are such shapes, with their islands and capes!
    But we've got our brave Captain to thank'
(So the crew would protest) 'that he's bought *us* the best –
    A perfect and absolute blank!'

This was charming, no doubt: but they shortly found out
    That the Captain they trusted so well
Had only one notion for crossing the ocean,
    And that was to tingle his bell.

He was thoughtful and grave – but the orders he gave
    Were enough to bewilder a crew.
When he cried 'Steer to starboard, but keep her head larboard!'
    What on earth was the helmsman to do?

Then the bowsprit got mixed with the rudder sometimes:
    A thing, as the Bellman remarked,
That frequently happens in tropical climes,
    When a vessel is, so to speak, 'snarked'.

But the principal failing occurred in the sailing,
    And the Bellman, perplexed and distressed,
Said he *had* hoped, at least, when the wind blew due East,
    That the ship would *not* travel due West!

But the danger was past – they had landed at last,
    With their boxes, portmanteaus, and bags:
Yet at first sight the crew were not pleased with the view
    Which consisted of chasms and crags.

The Bellman perceived that their spirits were low,
    And repeated in musical tone
Some jokes he had kept for a season of woe –
    But the crew would do nothing but groan.

He served out some grog with a liberal hand,
    And bade them sit down on the beach:
And they could not but own that their Captain looked grand,
    As he stood and delivered his speech.

'Friends, Romans, and countrymen, lend me your ears!'
    (They were all of them fond of quotations:
So they drank to his health, and they gave him three cheers,
    While he served out additional rations).

'We have sailed many months, we have sailed many weeks,
    (Four weeks to the month you may mark),
But never as yet ('tis your Captain who speaks)
    Have we caught the least glimpse of a Snark!

'We have sailed many weeks, we have sailed many days,
    (Seven days to the week I allow),
But a Snark, on the which we might lovingly gaze,
    We have never beheld till now!

'Come, listen, my men, while I tell you again
    The five unmistakable marks
By which you may know, wheresoever you go,
    The warranted genuine Snarks.

'Let us take them in order. The first is the taste,
    Which is meagre and hollow, but crisp:

Like a coat that is rather too tight in the waist,
   With a flavour of Will-o'-the-Wisp.

'Its habit of getting up late you'll agree
   That it carries too far, when I say
That it frequently breakfasts at five-o'clock tea,
   And dines on the following day.

'The third is its slowness in taking a jest.
   Should you happen to venture on one,
It will sigh like a thing that is deeply distressed:
   And it always looks grave at a pun.

'The fourth is its fondness for bathing-machines,
   Which it constantly carries about,
And believes that they add to the beauty of scenes –
   A sentiment open to doubt.

'The fifth is ambition. It next will be right
   To describe each particular batch:
Distinguishing those that have feathers, and bite,
   From those that have whiskers, and scratch.

'For, although common Snarks do no manner of harm;
   Yet I feel it my duty to say
Some are Boojums –' The Bellman broke off in alarm,
   For the Baker had fainted away.

FIT THE THIRD

The Baker's Tale

They roused him with muffins – they roused him with ice –
   They roused him with mustard and cress –
They roused him with jam and judicious advice –
   They set him conundrums to guess.

When at length he sat up and was able to speak,
   His sad story he offered to tell;
And the Bellman cried 'Silence! Not even a shriek!'
   And excitedly tingled his bell.

There was silence supreme! Not a shriek, not a scream,
  Scarcely even a howl or a groan,
As the man they called 'Ho!' told his story of woe
  In an antediluvian tone.

'My father and mother were honest, though poor –'
  'Skip all that!' cried the Bellman in haste.
'If it once becomes dark, there's no chance of a Snark –
  We have hardly a minute to waste!'

'I skip forty years,' said the Baker in tears,
  'And proceed without further remark
To the day when you took me aboard of your ship
  To help you in hunting the Snark.

'A dear uncle of mine (after whom I was named)
  Remarked, when I bade him farewell –'
'Oh, skip your dear uncle!' the Bellman exclaimed,
  As he angrily tingled his bell.

'He remarked to me then,' said that mildest of men,
  ' "If your Snark be a Snark, that is right:
Fetch it home by all means – you may serve it with greens
  And it's handy for striking a light.

' "You may seek it with thimbles – and seek it with care –
  You may hunt it with forks and hope;
You may threaten its life with a railway-share;
  You may charm it with smiles and soap –" '

('That's exactly the method,' the Bellman bold
  In a hasty parenthesis cried,
'That's exactly the way I have always been told
  That the capture of Snarks should be tried!')

' "But oh, beamish nephew, beware of the day,
  If your Snark be a Boojum! For then
You will softly and suddenly vanish away,
  And never be met with again!"

'It is this, it is this that oppresses my soul,
  When I think of my uncle's last words:

And my heart is like nothing so much as a bowl
　Brimming over with quivering curds!

'It is this, it is this –' 'We have had that before!'
　The Bellman indignantly said.
And the Baker replied 'Let me say it once more.
　It is this, it is this that I dread!

'I engage with the Snark – every night after dark –
　In a dreamy delirious fight:
I serve it with greens in those shadowy scenes,
　And I use it for striking a light:

'But if ever I meet with a Boojum, that day,
　In a moment (of this I am sure),
I shall softly and suddenly vanish away –
　And the notion I cannot endure!'

FIT THE FOURTH

The Hunting

The Bellman looked uffish, and wrinkled his brow.
　'If only you'd spoken before!
It's excessively awkward to mention it now,
　With the Snark, so to speak, at the door!

'We should all of us grieve, as you well may believe,
　If you never were met with again –
But surely, my man, when the voyage began,
　You might have suggested it then?

'It's excessively awkward to mention it now –
　As I think I've already remarked.'
And the man they called 'Hi!' replied, with a sigh,
　'I informed you the day we embarked.

'You may charge me with murder – or want of sense –
　(We are all of us weak at times):
But the slightest approach to a false pretence
　Was never among my crimes!

'I said it in Hebrew – I said it in Dutch –
　　I said it in German and Greek:
But I wholly forgot (and it vexes me much)
　　That English is what you speak!'

''Tis a pitiful tale,' said the Bellman, whose face
　　Had grown longer at every word:
'But, now that you've stated the whole of your case,
　　More debate would be simply absurd.

'The rest of my speech' (he exclaimed to his men)
　　'You shall hear when I've leisure to speak it.
But the Snark is at hand, let me tell you again!
　　'Tis your glorious duty to seek it!

'To seek it with thimbles, to seek it with care;
　　To pursue it with forks and hope;
To threaten its life with a railway-share;
　　To charm it with smiles and soap!

'For the Snark's a peculiar creature, that won't
　　Be caught in a commonplace way.
Do all that you know, and try all that you don't:
　　Not a chance must be wasted to–day!

'For England expects – I forbear to proceed:
　　'Tis a maxim tremendous, but trite:
And you'd best be unpacking the things that you need
　　To rig yourselves out for the fight.'

Then the Banker endorsed a blank cheque (which he crossed),
　　And changed his loose silver for notes:
The Baker with care combed his whiskers and hair,
　　And shook the dust out of his coats:

The Boots and the Broker were sharpening a spade –
　　Each working the grindstone in turn:
But the Beaver went on making lace, and displayed
　　No interest in the concern:

Though the Barrister tried to appeal to its pride,
　　And vainly proceeded to cite

A number of cases, in which making laces
   Had been proved an infringement of right.

The maker of Bonnets ferociously planned
   A novel arrangement of bows:
While the Billiard-marker with quivering hand
   Was chalking the tip of his nose.

But the Butcher turned nervous, and dressed himself fine,
   With yellow kid gloves and a ruff –
Said he felt it exactly like going to dine,
   Which the Bellman declared was all 'stuff'.

'Introduce me, now there's a good fellow,' he said,
   'If we happen to meet it together!'
And the Bellman, sagaciously nodding his head,
   Said 'That must depend on the weather.'

The Beaver went simply galumphing about,
   At seeing the Butcher so shy:
And even the Baker, though stupid and stout,
   Made an effort to wink with one eye.

'Be a man!' said the Bellman in wrath, as he heard
   The Butcher beginning to sob.
'Should we meet with a Jubjub, that desperate bird,
   We shall need all our strength for the job!'

FIT THE FIFTH

The Beaver's Lesson

They sought it with thimbles, they sought it with care;
   They pursued it with forks and hope;
They threatened its life with a railway-share;
   They charmed it with smiles and soap.

Then the Butcher contrived an ingenious plan
   For making a separate sally;
And had fixed on a spot unfrequented by man,
   A dismal and desolate valley.

But the very same plan to the Beaver occurred:
　　It had chosen the very same place:
Yet neither betrayed, by a sign or a word,
　　The disgust that appeared in his face.

Each thought he was thinking of nothing but 'Snark'
　　And the glorious work of the day;
And each tried to pretend that he did not remark
　　That the other was going that way.

But the valley grew narrower and narrower still,
　　And the evening got darker and colder,
Till (merely from nervousness, not from good will)
　　They marched along shoulder to shoulder.

Then a scream, shrill and high, rent the shuddering sky
　　And they knew that some danger was near:
The Beaver turned pale to the tip of its tail,
　　And even the Butcher felt queer.

He thought of his childhood, left far behind –
　　That blissful and innocent state –
The sound so exactly recalled to his mind
　　A pencil that squeaks on a slate!

'Tis the voice of the Jubjub!' he suddenly cried.
　　(This man, that they used to call 'Dunce'.)
'As the Bellman would tell you,' he added with pride,
　　'I have uttered that sentiment once.

''Tis the note of the Jubjub! Keep count, I entreat.
　　You will find I have told it you twice.
'Tis the song of the Jubjub! The proof is complete.
　　If only I've stated it thrice.'

The Beaver had counted with scrupulous care,
　　Attending to every word:
But it fairly lost heart, and outgrabe in despair,
　　When the third repetition occurred.

It felt that, in spite of all possible pains,
　　It had somehow contrived to lose count,

And the only thing now was to rack its poor brains
   By reckoning up the amount.

'Two added to one – if that could but be done',
   It said, 'with one's fingers and thumbs!'
Recollecting with tears how, in earlier years,
   It had taken no pains with its sums.

'The thing can be done,' said the Butcher, 'I think.
   The thing must be done, I am sure.
The thing shall be done! Bring me paper and ink,
   The best there is time to procure.'

The Beaver brought paper, portfolio, pens,
   And ink in unfailing supplies:
While strange creepy creatures came out of their dens,
   And watched them with wondering eyes.

So engrossed was the Butcher, he heeded them not,
   As he wrote with a pen in each hand,
And explained all the while in a popular style
   Which the Beaver could well understand.

'Taking Three as the subject to reason about –
   A convenient number to state –
We add Seven, and Ten, and then multiply out
   By One Thousand diminished by Eight.

'The result we proceed to divide, as you see,
   By Nine Hundred and Ninety and Two:
Then subtract Seventeen, and the answer must be
   Exactly and perfectly true.

'The method employed I would gladly explain,
   While I have it so clear in my head,
If I had but the time and you had but the brain –
   But much yet remains to be said.

'In one moment I've seen what has hitherto been
   Enveloped in absolute mystery,
And without extra charge I will give you at large
   A Lesson in Natural History.'

In his genial way he proceeded to say
   (Forgetting all laws of propriety,
And that giving instruction, without introduction,
   Would have caused quite a thrill in Society),

'As to temper the Jubjub's a desperate bird.
   Since it lives in perpetual passion:
Its taste in costume is entirely absurd –
   It is ages ahead of the fashion:

'But it knows any friend it has met once before:
   It never will look at a bribe:
And in charity-meetings it stands at the door,
   And collects – though it does not subscribe.

'Its flavour when cooked is more exquisite far
   Than mutton, or oysters, or eggs:
(Some think it keeps best in an ivory jar,
   And some, in mahogany kegs:)

'You boil it in sawdust: you salt it in glue:
   You condense it with locusts and tape:
Still keeping one principal object in view –
   To preserve its symmetrical shape.'

The Butcher would gladly have talked till next day,
   But he felt that the Lesson must end,
And he wept with delight in attempting to say
   He considered the Beaver his friend:

While the Beaver confessed, with affectionate looks
   More eloquent even than tears,
It had learned in ten minutes far more than all books
   Would have taught it in seventy years.

They returned hand-in-hand, and the Bellman, unmanned
   (For a moment) with noble emotion,
Said 'This amply repays all the wearisome days
   We have spent on the billowy ocean!'

Such friends, as the Beaver and Butcher became,
   Have seldom if ever been known;

In winter or summer, 'twas always the same –
    You could never meet either alone.

And when quarrels arose – as one frequently finds
    Quarrels will, spite of every endeavour –
The song of the Jubjub recurred to their minds,
    And cemented their friendship for ever!

FIT THE SIXTH

The Barrister's Dream

They sought it with thimbles, they sought it with care;
    They pursued it with forks and hope;
They threatened its life with a railway-share;
    They charmed it with smiles and soap.

But the Barrister, weary of proving in vain
    That the Beaver's lace-making was wrong,
Fell asleep, and in dreams saw the creature quite plain
    That his fancy had dwelt on so long.

He dreamed that he stood in a shadowy Court,
    Where the Snark, with a glass in its eye,
Dressed in gown, bands, and wig, was defending a pig
    On the charge of deserting its sty.

The Witnesses proved, without error or flaw,
    That the sty was deserted when found:
And the Judge kept explaining the state of the law
    In a soft under-current of sound.

The indictment had never been clearly expressed,
    And it seemed that the Snark had begun,
And had spoken three hours, before any one guessed
    What the pig was supposed to have done.

The Jury had each formed a different view
    (Long before the indictment was read),
And they all spoke at once, so that none of them knew
    One word that the others had said.

'You must know –' said the Judge: but the Snark exclaimed 'Fudge!
    That statute is obsolete quite!
Let me tell you, my friends, the whole question depends
    On an ancient manorial right.

'In the matter of Treason the pig would appear
    To have aided, but scarcely abetted:
While the charge of Insolvency fails, it is clear,
    If you grant the plea "never indebted".

'The fact of Desertion I will not dispute:
    But its guilt, as I trust, is removed
(So far as relates to the costs of this suit)
    By the Alibi which has been proved.

'My poor client's fate now depends on your votes.'
    Here the speaker sat down in his place,
And directed the Judge to refer to his notes
    And briefly to sum up the case.

But the Judge said he never had summed up before;
    So the Snark undertook it instead,
And summed it so well that it came to far more
    Than the Witnesses ever had said!

When the verdict was called for, the Jury declined,
    As the word was so puzzling to spell;
But they ventured to hope that the Snark wouldn't mind
    Undertaking that duty as well.

So the Snark found the verdict, although, as it owned,
    It was spent with the toils of the day:
When it said the word 'GUILTY!' the Jury all groaned
    And some of them fainted away.

Then the Snark pronounced sentence, the Judge being quite
    Too nervous to utter a word:
When it rose to its feet, there was silence like night,
    And the fall of a pin might be heard.

'Transportation for life' was the sentence it gave,
    'And *then* to be fined forty pound.'

The Jury all cheered, though the Judge said he feared
   That the phrase was not legally sound.

But their wild exultation was suddenly checked
   When the jailer informed them, with tears,
Such a sentence would have not the slightest effect,
   As the pig had been dead for some years.

The Judge left the Court, looking deeply disgusted
   But the Snark, though a little aghast,
As the lawyer to whom the defence was intrusted,
   Went bellowing on to the last.

Thus the Barrister dreamed, while the bellowing seemed
   To grow every moment more clear:
Till he woke to the knell of a furious bell,
   Which the Bellman rang close at his ear.

FIT THE SEVENTH

The Banker's Fate

They sought it with thimbles, they sought it with care;
   They pursued it with forks and hope;
They threatened its life with a railway-share;
   They charmed it with smiles and soap.

And the Banker, inspired with a courage so new
   It was matter for general remark,
Rushed madly ahead and was lost to their view
   In his zeal to discover the Snark.

But while he was seeking with thimbles and care,
   A Bandersnatch swiftly drew nigh
And grabbed at the Banker, who shrieked in despair,
   For he knew it was useless to fly.

He offered large discount – he offered a cheque
   (Drawn 'to bearer') for seven-pounds-ten:
But the Bandersnatch merely extended its neck
   And grabbed at the Banker again.

Without rest or pause – while those frumious jaws
    Went savagely snapping around –
He skipped and he hopped, and he floundered and flopped,
    Till fainting he fell to the ground.

The Bandersnatch fled as the others appeared
    Led on by that fear-stricken yell:
And the Bellman remarked 'It is just as I feared!'
    And solemnly tolled on his bell.

He was black in the face, and they scarcely could trace
    The least likeness to what he had been:
While so great was his fright that his waistcoat turned white –
    A wonderful thing to be seen!

To the horror of all who were present that day,
    He uprose in full evening dress,
And with senseless grimaces endeavoured to say
    What his tongue could no longer express.

Down he sank in a chair – ran his hands through his hair –
    And chanted in mimsiest tones
Words whose utter inanity proved his insanity,
    While he rattled a couple of bones.

'Leave him here to his fate – it is getting so late!'
    The Bellman exclaimed in a fright.
'We have lost half the day. Any further delay,
    And we sha'n't catch a Snark before night!'

FIT THE EIGHTH

The Vanishing

They sought it with thimbles, they sought it with care;
    They pursued it with forks and hope;
They threatened its life with a railway-share;
    They charmed it with smiles and soap.

They shuddered to think that the chase might fail,
    And the Beaver, excited at last,

Went bounding along on the tip of its tail,
　　For the daylight was nearly past.

'There is Thingumbob shouting!' the Bellman said.
　　'He is shouting like mad, only hark!
He is waving his hands, he is wagging his head,
　　He has certainly found a Snark!'

They gazed in delight, while the Butcher exclaimed
　　'He was always a desperate wag!'
They beheld him – their Baker – their hero unnamed –
　　On the top of a neighbouring crag,

Erect and sublime, for one moment of time,
　　In the next, that wild figure they saw
(As if stung by a spasm) plunge into a chasm,
　　While they waited and listened in awe.

'It's a Snark!' was the sound that first came to their ears,
　　And seemed almost too good to be true.
Then followed a torrent of laughter and cheers:
　　Then the ominous words 'It's a Boo –'

Then, silence. Some fancied they heard in the air
　　A weary and wandering sigh
That sounded like '–jum!' but the others declare
　　It was only a breeze that went by.

They hunted till darkness came on, but they found
　　Not a button, or feather, or mark,
By which they could tell that they stood on the ground
　　Where the Baker had met with the Snark.

In the midst of the word he was trying to say,
　　In the midst of his laughter and glee,
He had softly and suddenly vanished away –
　　For the Snark *was* a Boojum, you see.

LEWIS CARROLL

PENGUIN POPULAR CLASSICS

Published or forthcoming

PENGUIN POPULAR CLASSICS

Published or forthcoming

PENGUIN POPULAR CLASSICS

Published or forthcoming

George Grossmith	The Diary of a Nobody
Brothers Grimm	Grimm's Fairy Tales
H. Rider Haggard	Allan Quatermain
	King Solomon's Mines
Thomas Hardy	Far from the Madding Crowd
	Jude the Obscure
	The Mayor of Casterbridge
	A Pair of Blue Eyes
	The Return of the Native
	Tess of the D'Urbervilles
	The Trumpet-Major
	Under the Greenwood Tree
	The Woodlanders
Nathaniel Hawthorne	The Scarlet Letter
Anthony Hope	The Prisoner of Zenda
Thomas Hughes	Tom Brown's Schooldays
Victor Hugo	The Hunchback of Notre-Dame
Henry James	The Ambassadors
	The American
	The Aspern Papers
	Daisy Miller
	The Europeans
	The Portrait of a Lady
	The Turn of the Screw
	Washington Square
M. R. James	Ghost Stories
Jerome K. Jerome	Three Men in a Boat
	Three Men on the Bummel
James Joyce	Dubliners
	A Portrait of the Artist as a Young Man
Charles Kingsley	The Water Babies
Rudyard Kipling	Captains Courageous
	The Jungle Books
	Just So Stories
	Kim
	Plain Tales from the Hills
	Puck of Pook's Hill

PENGUIN POPULAR CLASSICS

Published or forthcoming

PENGUIN POPULAR CLASSICS

Published or forthcoming

PENGUIN POPULAR POETRY

Published or forthcoming

The Selected Poems *of:*

Matthew Arnold
William Blake
Robert Browning
Robert Burns
Lord Byron
John Donne
Thomas Hardy
John Keats
Rudyard Kipling
Alexander Pope
Alfred Tennyson
William Wordsworth
William Yeats

and collections of:

Seventeenth-Century Poetry
Eighteenth-Century Poetry
Poetry of the Romantics
Victorian Poetry
Twentieth-Century Poetry
Scottish Folk and Fairy Tales